THE HEART OF THE ELEMENTS

FIRE'S FURY

notionpress
.com

THE HEART OF THE ELEMENTS

FIRE'S FURY

SHARADA M SUBRAHMANYAM

notionpress.com

Notion Press

Old No. 38, New No. 6,

McNichols Road, Chetpet,

Chennai - 600 031

First Published by Notion Press 2015

ISBN: 978-93-52060-61-0

PROLOGUE

In order to understand the story that shall be told, one must first delve into the past and understand the history behind it, for, if the right decisions are taken, patterns repeat themselves, and thus, the future can be predicted. To understand the pattern, let us go back several millennia to the time when the universe was born.

In the beginning, the universe was far spread; it was everywhere, and yet nowhere; it was colorful, yet grey; it was everything, yet nothing. This was the origin of our universe – Chaos. Chaos was the epitome of differences and unity; it was the essence of who we are now.

And so it was that many years later – if time existed in such a place – that Chaos separated into five beings: Earth; solid and homely; Air, life-giving and clear; Water; pure and flowing; fire, fierce and consuming; and Ether, mysterious and abstruse. These beings were the Elements, and they represented different parts of Chaos.

Now, the Elements protected one another and gave each other help when they needed it. They decided upon an arrangement to ensure them the utmost protection. Earth went first. She was solid, and gave the others a place to rest. Water went next. She needed a place to flow in order to survive, for otherwise, she would be one with Air. So, Water lay on Earth and flowed freely. Next came Air. He covered both Earth and Water to give them protection from the remaining Chaos and ensure that they would not dissolve as he had. Ether followed his brother and surrounded them, for he was vast and never ending. Fire embedded herself in Ether, giving the other elements Light and Color. And so, for many years, they lived together in harmony, protecting each other from Chaos, who was trying as hard as he could to become whole again.

There soon came a time when Chaos accepted defeat, and let himself be divided amongst his children. The Elements, for a short period, continued living as they had been those many years. But soon, one became restless and yearned for more. Fire, all consuming, thought that she was not dependent on anyone, and so attacked her siblings. She sent from her Pyrós powerful bolts of fire towards the others, and tried to consume them. Earth, Air, and Water retaliated, and the universe began dissolving. And so, it seemed that even after his defeat, Chaos would still win.

Then, when he saw his brother and sisters were almost completely dispersed, Ether came forth. Upon his entrance, the other Elements paused, stunned. They had never thought about their weakening, and when Ether came, they were reminded of their true power. Fire, ashamed of her greed, threw down her Pyrós. The others soon followed suit, with Earth dropping her Gis, Air tossing his Astrapí, and Water dropping her Kÿma.

Then, Ether said, "'Tis without knowing that we fought. We must be more careful now. Let us have peacekeepers, ones who will help us avoid future conflicts." The others agreed, and so they created life. All the People they created had all the Elements, but only one group knew how to use them – the Humans. They used water and air to travel and survive, fire to keep warm and cook food, and earth to store food and rest. Only Ether was not used by any of the People. The People lived for long and did their duty, but Ether kept to himself his father's last words – "Your creations shall bring you your doom." Since only Ether heard these words, he assumed that only his creations would bring their fall. He thus refrained from contributing to the People, but unknown to him, a small part of his mysteriousness became part of the People.

CHAPTER I

"And that, children, is the story of the Elements," concluded Mr. Alwood. Galene had heard the story a million times, and was bored. *And then comes the question,* she thought.

"But grandfather, which of the People had Ether's mysteriousness?"

And there it was. This question came every time, and each time, Mr. Alwood said, "We are not sure, child. We would know if Ether had known, I suppose."

Galene sighed. *Like we know everything that the Elements knew!* She thought. Then she got up and stretched. "Thanks, Grandpa. We need to go to school now. C'mon, Melete. Let's get moving." Galene reached out to her sister.

Galene. It meant calm, and it couldn't be further from her personality. She was, by nature, fiery and adventurous, and their mother used to tell them that Galene ought to have been named differently.

Melete, on the other hand, meant ponder, and ponder she would. Melete would think her actions through, and then do it. She was the exact opposite of her sister.

The sisters walked to school, and as usual, were not disturbed by the cold. Melete liked to joke that it was Galene's fiery personality, but the older redhead felt it was more. She didn't know how right she was, but when she did, she wished she had been wrong.

"Hi, Gale! Hey, Melete!"

Galene looked up and smiled. "Hey, Caelus."

Melete slipped her hand out of Galene's. "See you, Galene." She had spotted some of her friends.

Galene nodded. "Bye, Melete."

She had barely turned around when she was ambushed by three of her other friends. "Gale!" Squealed Aura, throwing her arms around her. *The way she reacted when she saw me,* thought Galene, *you'd think she'd seen me a century ago.*

Galene slipped out of Aura's grasp, and said, "Hi, Aura, Dhar, Dessie."

Perhaps a bit more about them, before the story moves on. Aura was a quite hyper girl. She had pale skin and even paler hair, if that were possible, and electric blue eyes. She was rather tall, but was by no means the tallest of the group. That position was taken by Caelus. He was unpredictable but loyal, and had greyish blue eyes and black hair. He had a brilliant sense of humor, but the trouble was, according to him, no one else found his jokes funny.

Dhara was an Indian, and he was rather quiet. He had black hair and dark brown eyes, and was the second shortest of the group. The shortest was Despione, who preferred to be called Dessie, and would react rather strongly to anyone calling her Despione (and that was an understatement). Only the teachers called her that, and she found it rather unhealthy for her grades to make a fuss about her name with the teachers. She had black hair and black eyes, and was rather quiet. But don't let that fool you. She was rather cunning, and nearly always got her way. And the thing is, you won't even know that she had maneuvered the situation to favor her.

"Hi, Gale," Dhara and Dessie said. "Hey, Caelus."

"Sup!" Caelus said.

"The sky!" The rest of them chorused.

"Hey, you copied me!" He accused. Galene rolled her eyes.

"Get used to it." She said, and the others laughed at her mock seriousness. The group joked about until the bell rang, after which they went to their classes.

Galene went to her locker and glanced at her timetable. She groaned.

"What?" Dessie asked.

"Social first, followed by gym." Galene groaned.

Dessie smiled. "Well, get the boring things over with first, right?" Galene glared at her and refused to answer. Dessie just laughed.

Galene dragged herself to class. Unfortunately, she was late. "Miss Alwood, why can you not get to class in time?" Mrs. Ackerly demanded.

"Sorry, Mrs. Ackerly." Galene mumbled. "It won't happen again." Mrs. Ackerly pursed her lips and nodded. Galene went in and sat with Dhara.

He passed her a note. *Way to annoy Mrs. Ackerly again.*

She glared at him. *I don't do it on purpose.*

Dhara just smiled. Galene, being a model of maturity, decided to stick her tongue out at Dhara.

The rest of the day passed without much event, with the small exception of someone mixing the wrong chemicals in the lab. Galene met her friends and her sister, and together, they went home, laughing, joking, and generally having fun.

Little did they know that it would not last long.

Galene stuck her head in her grandfather's room. "You called, Grandpa?"

Mr. Alwood looked up. "Ah, yes. Galene. Come in. Sit."

He sounded a bit flustered, and kept fidgeting with a small charm. *He's nervous,* Galene noted.

"What did you want to talk to me about?" Galene asked, honestly curious. Mr. Alwood rarely let anyone into his study, and for anyone to be called in was unheard of.

Mr. Alwood paused, seemingly collecting his thoughts. Finally he said, "Tell me about your friends. Caelus, Aura, Dhara, Despione."

Galene frowned, mind whirling. What did he need that for? Regardless, she told Mr. Alwood, "Caelus is humorous, I guess. He thinks so, at any rate. He's rather unpredictable. He's very protective as well."

"Aura." Mr. Alwood interlocked his fingers.

Galene raised her eyebrows, but continued. "Aura's most striking characteristic is her loyalty, I guess. She's light hearted, and loves talking. She's rather girly, truth be told." She added as an afterthought. "Dhara's quiet, but not as quiet as Dessie."

"Dessie?" Mr. Alwood interrupted.

"Despione. She hates being ca- I mean, she dislikes being called Despione. Dhara's steady and calm, but when he gets angry, it's like watching a volcano explode." Mr. Alwood paled at these words, but Galene didn't notice. She was busy recalling the one time she'd seen Dhara angry. "Despione – well, I've never seen her angry. She's the quietest, and almost always easy to overlook," here Galene shrugs, "except when she isn't. It's sort of hard to explain. It's like-"

"Something that you know you'll never see again, except you do." Mr. Alwood said quietly.

Galene looked at Mr. Alwood, surprised. "Exactly. How did you-"

"Bring them here tomorrow. I need to meet them."

Galene started, surprised, but nodded. She would find out tomorrow anyway.

And she turned around and left.

CHAPTER 2

"Enter!" called a voice. Galene glanced at her friends, and pushed the door open.

"Grandpa," Galene started, stepping forward. "This is-"

"I know." He pursed his lips. "Caelus. Aura. Dhara. Despione." He pointed to each of them in turn.

"How did you know?" Galene glanced at Mr. Alwood, confused.

"Don't call me Despione," Dessie grumbled.

Grandpa looked at her coolly. "That is your name, is it not, Miss Griffon?"

"Yes, but I prefer Dessie."

Mr. Alwood ignored her protest and turned to Galene. "As for how I know, well, that's why I called you here." The teens waited in silence. "Sit," sighed Mr. Alwood. "This is a long story." He waited until they sat, and began. "What do you know of the Elements?"

Galene and Caelus exchanged glances. "Whatever you've told us, sir. We know the stories."

Mr. Alwood nodded, unsurprised. "The Elements as you know, passed on some of their powers to each their creations. What most people don't know is that in each generation, five people are born who can actually control it. Not in the way humans have, but actual control. The power is like a flame inside them, waiting to be released."

"Why five, sir?" Dhara asked in his deep voice.

"The stories have something wrong. Ether knows that some of his powers went into the People. However, he made sure that his power was seen only in a few people. One of them is, for lack of a better word, his heir.

"Now, the five people who can control the Elements are called, as you have no doubt guessed, the Elements' Heirs. They can be anybody – no one knows who it might be next. However, there are a few characteristics that they have in common. The Finthé Heirs, Heirs of Earth, usually have dark hair and brown eyes. They have a calm demeanor, but can get violently upset. The Vrar Heirs, heirs of Air, have light hair and electric blue eyes. They aren't very easily distinguished personality-wise from the other humans. They are, however, strikingly loyal. The Hedra Heirs, heirs of water, have bluish-gray eyes, like those of the ocean deeps. They have wavy black hair, and are exceedingly protective. The Ethella Heirs are quiet and usually unremarkable, except when they aren't." Here Mr. Alwood smiled at Galene. "I assume you told them of our conversation." She nodded. "The Pyra Heirs, heirs of fire, are usually redheads, and have golden eyes. Their tempers are unmatched. Their's is a fighting spirit, and they never give up." Mr. Alwood leaned back.

"So you're saying that we're the Elements' Heirs?" Galene asked, incredulous. Mr. Alwood nodded.

"Prove it." Aura's normally light voice was dead serious.

Mr. Alwood raised his eyebrows. Aura crossed her arms in an 'I'm waiting' sort of a gesture. Mr. Alwood extended his arm. A ball of fire popped into existence above his palm, dancing up his arm.

Galene stiffened. All those incidents…She'd been burning things when she got excited, lighting them up and sending their sparks up to heaven. She walked towards her grandfather and extended her own arm. She focused, and sparks flew, literally. The two blazes joined, and danced together wildly. Gold met gold, and, for a moment, the fire heightened. Galene tilted her head, sending a silent message to her grandfather. *Thank you.*

He understood.

Mr. Alwood turned to Aura. "Proof enough?"

"Yessir." She said, seemingly awed. Galene internally groaned. Aura was probably freaking out on the inside. She'd be impossible to talk to for the next few days.

Galene turned back to Mr. Alwood, confused. Why did she have the powers? Why did the rest of them have the powers. She opened her mouth to ask the questions.

"It's not exactly powers. Everybody has the Magic, but only a few can use it. You five can. It's my job to teach you how."

"What about the other Heirs?" Dessie asked, tilting her head.

Mr. Alwood's face grew pained. "They died." He said shortly, pursing his lips. "When an Heir dies, his or her powers, for lack of a better word, gets passed on to the Heir he or she was closest to. So right now, I have all the powers. My power was originally Pyra's, and so my eye color and attitude didn't change much."

There was a brief, and surprisingly comfortable, pause. Dhara broke the silence. "When do we start?"

Mr. Alwood smiled without humor. "Now."

Galene flopped onto her bed, exhausted. *That was tough,* she thought. Her muscles were – well, on fire would be the wrong phrase. *Fire,* she mulled over the thought, letting it fill her mind. *It makes sense,* she finally settled. She always felt calm gazing into the fire, watching the colors play around. Melete always said –

She bolted upright. *Melete!* What would she do? *If what grandpa said is true, then-*

She shook her head. She'd think about that when the time came.

Fire… She came back to the original thought. It felt so natural, so light, so…free.

And Caelus is Water. She still didn't know how to think about that. Water and Fire. She always felt comfortable around him, but now…

Don't be stupid. She berated herself. *He treated you no differently in training today.*

No, a small voice niggled the back of her head. *He did distance himself…*

She shook her head again. *Stop it,* she told herself. *Nothing happened.*

She closed her eyes, and slowly, let the warm blanket of sleep cover her.

CHAPTER 3

The next morning, Galene got up, feeling down. *Why- oh.* The previous day's events crashed down, and her shoulders sagged. She sighed, and got ready for school. Just as she was going down, however, Melete ran into her.

"Gale! Grandpa says you can't go to school! Why?" She cried.

Galene froze up. "What?" She narrowed her eyes, and stormed up to Mr. Alwood's study. She opened the door, and went in, without waiting for acknowledgement.

"What did you do?" She demanded, her voice shaking in anger.

"Pulled you out. The Principal knows about the situation."

"You had no right!" She yelled, furious. "You didn't even tell me! Why can't I go, anyway?"

Mr. Alwood looked up. "I had every right," he said coolly. "You're developing your 'powers', and at this stage in training, your control is fleeting. It's better-"

"Better?!" She shouted. "There is no way it's *better*!"

"§*There is. You have very little control.*§"

"§*I have much more control than you know!*§" Before Galene could continue, however, Aura interrupted.

"What was that?" She looked at Galene.

"That," Mr. Alwood said, "was Pyropathos."

"What are you talking about?" Galene demanded irritably. "And what are you doing here?"

"I've come for training, of course." Aura said in a *that-should-be-obvious* tone.

"Pyropathos, or Fire-speech, is one of the powers that comes with being a Pyra's Heir. In a way, we talk to fire, whisper to it. It responds to us, crackling back, I suppose. Pyra's Heirs have a natural ability to understand it."

Whispers? Galene nearly blinked. *I don't whisper, but the fire does.* She remembered all the times when she sat in front of the fire, listening to the tongues hiss their words, sing their songs, dance to a music that only they could hear.

Except she could too.

She never told anybody, but she assumed Mr. Alwood knew, and glared at him. *Isn't there anything about me that he doesn't know?*

She turned to Aura. "You got pulled out too?"

"Yeah." She waved a hand dismissively. "This is better than school anyway."

Galene was interrupted for the second time that day. "Hey, girls!" Galene turned, ready to verbally burn the person who came in for interrupting her *again*.

"Why- Oh. Caelus." Galene froze, words dying in her throat.

"You don't seem happy to see me." He raised his eyebrows teasingly.

"You decided it was a good idea to come in and interrupt me when I was going to verbally *burn* Aura, and then say, 'you don't seem happy to see me'?"

"Pardon me, lady Hestia."

Galene raised her eyebrows. "Lady Hestia?"

Caelus grinned. "Greek goddess of fire, also known as Vesta."

Galene grinned, temper forgotten. He didn't hate her! "The world is about to end! Caelus has learnt about an ancient god!"

Caelus scowled playfully. "Quiet, you."

Just then, Dhar and Dessie came in. "Hey!" They said simultaneously in greeting.

Galene rolled her eyes. "Practicing twin speech, are we?"

"Nope!" They said together again.

"Doesn't seem like it."

They shrugged. Galene turned to Caelus, who mysteriously started shaking, like he was trying not to laugh or cry. Judging by the way his eyes were twinkling, Galene decided to go with laughing.

"What?" Galene asked quietly.

"A little trick I asked your grandfather about. It annoys them when the other says the same thing as they do. Watch." Galene turned back to the pair, but didn't have time to observe, as Mr. Alwood decided to begin the lesson then.

"Well, then, let's see what you've got." Mr. Alwood smiled.

And so it began.

The Heir's training continued with little mishap, and soon, it was the last training session, though the teens didn't know it.

Galene glanced at the other Heirs. They'd changed a lot the past few months. They had all shot up in height, and well muscled. Though the muscles didn't seem like much, well, woe to those who crossed them. Their individual characteristics changed as well.

Aura's eyes could have earlier passed as light blue, but now, they were impossible to overlook.

They were a striking, electric blue, with flecks of grey that came when she was especially angry. Her hair, already fair, became fairer, and she almost seemed like a fairy – a strong, hot tempered one at that.

With Dhara, it was the exact opposite. His eyes became darker, almost black, but lightened when he was in a good mood, which, considering, happened often enough. His hair became darker, if that was possible; it was black as midnight.

Despione had changed little, except that she was even better at blending in than before. However, when you make her mad, well, it got more than a little creepy. Her eyes got flecks of silver in them, and it almost looked like she got the sky in her eyes – if the sky had only shooting stars. Galene had the misfortune to experience that, and she'd been *very* careful since.

Caelus… well, she tried not to think about him. She tended to burn things when she did (no, she did not like him). But Caelus had changed as well. When she looked into his eyes, she felt like she was in the river, then the sea, then deep in the ocean – shades so striking that she felt lost in them (again, no, she did not like him. Stop asking!). His hair became wavy, like the soft ripples caused by a small fish swimming below the surface of a still lake, and took a slight brownish tinge, so faint that it almost couldn't be seen. But it was there, and hard for the Heirs to miss.

As for Galene herself, well, she could see the differences easily. Perhaps it was because she knew herself best, but the fact remained that she could. Her eyes became warmer, like the flames in a fireplace. It would, when she was in a good mood, flicker like the soft flames in the grate during a cold winter evening, warm and inviting. However, when she was angry, her friends told her, they would flash like a piece of firewood dipped in gasoline – quick, fiery, and destructive. Her hair became less curly and more wavy, but not nearly as wavy as Caelus'. His was the softest (and waviest) of the lot.

But the Heirs changed in ways other than physically. Their control over their Elements increased dramatically, and new ones were discovered. It seemed that Galene had Pyropathos, the ability to converse with fire. She held long 'conversations' with flames from various places, and it was interesting, to say the least. Caelus had Hedravista, the ability to converse with creatures of the water. As far as Galene knew, Hedra's Heirs couldn't speak with water the way Pyra's heirs could speak to fire, but there was always a first. Caelus didn't seem to like it, though. Aura had Vrarora, the ability to speak with creatures of the air. Once she even called a few of her feathery friends inside the training room, much to Mr. Alwood's annoyance, and Galene's amusement. Dhara had Finthspíez, the ability to speak to creatures of the Earth. Their conversations looked very odd, as he didn't need to open his mouth to 'talk' to them. Despione had Ethelova, the ability to speak to the skies. This, the heirs felt, was a bit helpful, in that they could always tell exactly where they were.

Apart from all of this (yes, there's more!), the heirs were all fluent in Lenaula, the language of the Elements. It took them a while to learn, but they did, and it was satisfactory, if not anything else.

"Gather round, Heleanova[1]," called Mr. Alwood, pulling Galene from her train of thought. The Heirs approached him cautiously. The last time he'd done this was to teach them to never let their guard down. It wasn't pretty, to say the least.

"Yes, Grandpa?"

Mr. Alwood took a deep breath. "Your training is now over. To quote a cliché that is more than appropriate here, my work here is done."

1 Heirs

CHAPTER 4

There was a brief pause, in which Galene's mind slowed. *Work is done?* She thought. Mr. Alwood couldn't possibly be leaving, could he? Where would he go?

The other Heleanova gave her sympathetic glances, and she slowly understood. She felt herself growing numb, and a hard, emotionless mask slipped onto her face. The mask she wore when something goes wrong… The mask she wore in the Principal's office when she found her parents had died, and her grandfather was going to raise herself and her sister. …The mask she wore when she was bullied… The mask…

"I'm sorry, Galene." Mr. Alwood said, his voice soft, gentle.

"Melete?" Galene heard herself say, her voice sounding cold even to herself.

"Your aunt will take care of her."

She nodded, and turned to her training area. She raised her hand. A white-hot torrent of fire flew from her hand, burning the target she was aiming for. And the next. And the next. She went on torching things, her mask never leaving her face. And if a few tears slipped through the mask, nobody said anything.

Alone. Galene stared at the sky, the blanket that now meant so much to the world, and yet so little to her. A lone tear traced its way down her cheek. *Alone.* She was alone. Everyone had left soon after she started torching things, and she hadn't realized it. They had left her, and her grandfather was going to leave her. Even Melete would be leaving her soon…

She leaned back onto the mattress she'd dragged to the terrace, another tear following the first.

Abruptly, she flipped around and screamed silently into her pillow. *Why? Why does he have to go?* She raged silently, her tears running freely now. Though she had never admitted it, her grandfather had been a lifesaver. He'd slowly brought her back to normal, helping her get over her sorrow and pain. And now, there was no one.

"A nice sight you are, moping like this."

Immediately, Galene snapped into a defensive position, her arm raised to attack. Another hand grabbed it before she could, and Galene blinked.

Oh.

"Hi guys," she muttered dejectedly.

"Move over." Aura and Dessie said simultaneously. Galene complied, too depressed to notice the annoyed glance that Dessie sent Aura.

The hand holding hers let go. Galene turned to the owner of the hand, Caelus. "Sorry, Cal."

Caelus waved his hand. "It's nothing. You didn't burn me or anything."

"I could've!"

"But you didn't." Caelus slid down onto the mattress, Dhara following suit. "We startled you. We shouldn't have done that."

Galene leaned onto Aura's shoulder. "How did you get here anyway? I didn't hear the bell."

Caelus glanced at Aura. She shook her head. Galene noticed, and turned. "You flew them here?" Galene asked, surprised. She'd flat out refused to let anyone else fly with her.

Aura shook her head, but when everyone else glared at her, she nodded sheepishly. Galene put her head in her hands. "Sorry. You didn't have to."

Dessie put her hands on her hips. "Of course we didn't have to. We should have just let you mope and moan by yourself, because that's what friends do. We leave our friend alone when she needs us the most. Yeah right!"

Galene raised her eyebrows. Then she slumped her shoulders and sighed. "Thanks."

The girls took this as a signal for them to sit. Dessie took Galene's hands in her own, and Aura rubbed circles in Galene's back. "Talk to me, Gale," Dessie whispered softly. Galene looked into Dessie's eyes, and opened her mouth.

And promptly began crying.

She didn't know how long she cried, what she said, why she was doing this – she just did. She cried and cried and cried, shoulders shaking from the effort of holding back for so long.

Finally, after an eternity, she wiped her eyes, and sat up. "I just can't believe he's going. I thought-" she broke off, confused, angry, sad, all at once. "I don't know what I thought."

"It's alright. He's accepted it."

Galene nodded. She stood up and turned to the others. "We don't have long now. We're going to have to start soon."

Dhara nodded. "I've done some research-"

"Of course." Caelus interrupted.

Dhara shot him a look. "Each of us will be given a tool, something that will help us in our journey."

There was a pause. "And what tools are they?" Aura asked.

Dhara grinned. "Our weapons."

Galene crept down to her grandfather's room. She hesitated, rocking on her heels, and then knocked the door. "Come in, Galene."

She closed the door softly behind her. "How did you know that it was me?"

Mr. Alwood smiled. "I can sense the heirs, and each of you give out a different 'scent', for lack of a better word."

Galene nodded, and bit her lip. "How-" she hesitated. "How much longer?"

His eyes softened, looking much like the warm hearth on a cold winter's day. "Any time now."

She moved closer, and knelt next to his bed, where he was lying down. "I'll miss you."

He raised his eyebrows. "And I you."

There was a comfortable silence. Suddenly, her eyes snapped up. "Why?" She whispered. He understood.

Mr. Alwood smiled softly. "That is the way of things. But I'll never be truly gone. The legacy, The Heleanovan Legacy, its never truly gone. There will always be Heleanova, and they are the true legacy, the true carriers of the past. The Heleanova spread the awareness, the belief that the Elements are there, that they exist, that they help. The awareness is subtle, travelling from the children, who believe anything, to the adults, seldom believing, but somehow, quietly, they remember their childhood stories, tales, beliefs. You must carry that on. You must spread the knowledge, the belief, and most importantly, the hope. The hope that even in the darkest of situations, things can only get better, that there is nothing else that will hurt us anymore, that we are, truly, united by the Elements."

She pressed his hand to her heart, and looked into his eyes. "Stay with me."

He nodded. "Forever."

And just like that, he was gone.

CHAPTER 5

"I did some research," began Dhara.

"Again," interrupted Caelus.

Dhara shot him a look. "The weapons shift form based on what we are like. They finally settle at the end of the training, when we begin our First Journey."

"And I suppose," Galene said, "that you know what the forms are?"

Dhara smiled. "I figured it out," he said, looking smug.

There was a pause. "Tell us, Dhar." Aura sat forward, eager.

"For Caelus, the Hedra Helianov, The Kÿma. The Weapon of Water. Yours will be a sword, as you are most comfortable with fighting close range, A sword will give you that. Also, it suits your personality: your fighting style is unpredictable, much like you, and with a sword, you are even more so.

"For you, Galene, Pyra Helianov, The Pyrós. A knife, suiting your style, to come close and bite. You are subtle, sneaky, and come up with methods to surprise us that we would have never thought of ourselves.

"Aura, Vrar Helianov, you have the bow and arrow, The Astrapí. Long range. You take out your enemies when they least expect you, with the winds always blowing in your favor. I expect that even in the windiest of days, you will never miss your target. Especially on the windiest of days.

"Myself, Finthé Helianov, The Gis. A spear. Straightforward, but nigh impossible to evade or defeat, except by the true masters. It will be exceptionally easy for me to master most weapons, because, directly or indirectly, they come from the earth.

"And finally, Despione. Ethella Helianov, Heir of Ether. The Caelum. Yours, I expect, is the greatest surprise of all. You have disks, used both for long and short range, designed to take out your enemies with a single throw. You are mysterious, difficult to figure out, the most cunning of us all. The disks are designed so that it will be impossible to find out where they came from. They will be, in other words, completely you."

There was a brief pause, as everybody imagined their weapons. Galene smiled to herself. *Just as I thought.* She had done some research as well. Time to reveal her own work.

"I did some research too." She brought out her notepad. "The weapons are hidden in places where the power of the Elements are high. The Kÿma will be found in the ocean, where the power of the ocean is unrivaled. The other Elements will also have to be present, so it will probably be in an underwater volcano, contained in a bubble of air, to prevent it from falling into disrepair. It will have pale green blade, a bit like sea green, but not quite there. The hilt will be a slightly darker green, and studded with emeralds. The sheath will be green – pure, undiluted green. It will have a silver band to keep it with the green belt, which will have a silver buckle. It will have by its side a pearl, containing his locked power, to be unleashed when we all have ours.

"The Pyrós will be found in a volcano. It will have a triangular blade, with fire patterns, almost like the blade itself is on fire. The hilt will be orange-red, with a studded ruby. The sheath will be red, with a gold band to hold it to the belt, red in color with a gold buckle. It will have by its side a fire opal, with my locked power.

"The Astrapí will have a silvery white bow with a black string. It will have a stormy gray quiver, with the arrows a darker gray, with a lighter tip and fletching. At the bottom of the quiver, there will be line of star sapphires. It will be found in a hurricane in the middle of the ocean, with the sun beating down and a bit of earth added to the mix. The locked power will be in white moonstone.

"The Gis will be found underground, in a cavern lit by Magical fire and protected by a storm of air and water. It will be made of platinum, and will have a diamond tip. Pure, untainted, as the Elements wished for it to be. His locked power will be in a crystal of silver topaz.

"The Caelum will be found when all others have been. Ether went through special ways to ensure that his heir is true. Nothing else is available about its location. Each will be a three bladed disk, seamless and whole. They will be in shades of violet, with an amethyst at the center, reflecting your mystery. Your locked power will be in a purple zircon."

There was another pause. Then Caelus joked, "Looks like she outdid you, Dhar."

The other heirs burst out laughing at the look on Dhara's face. "At least she did something. You lot, on the other hand…"

He let his voice taper off. The heirs stopped laughing long enough to look appropriately contrite, and promptly started laughing again. Dhara shook his head. "Hopeless, the lot of you."

And so, the five friends gathered their belongings, and set off on a journey that would change everything.

Chapter 6

"Where can they be?" Galene was biting her lips in frustration. The Heleanova had tried everything, even reaching out with their magical senses to try to detect their weapons. They came up with nothing. The technique, Mr. Alwood had said, was an obscure one, but would, for sure, yield results. The fact that they couldn't detect them either meant that the weapons were hidden by magic, or that they were in another layer of reality, another dimension, altogether. The latter was an alarming possibility, since none of them knew the slightest of what they might find there. The scary thing was that this was the more likely one, since it took them days of digging to find even a hint of a spell to find the spell to hide magical traces, and even that would leave a trace. Though only the Helianov can perform true magic, every human had a small amount of power in them. There were so many magical traces all over the world that no one knew where to start.

Finally, Dessie dropped the book that she had in her hands on the table. Ignoring Dhara's scandalized look, she said, "We all should concentrate on the Pyrós. Its protective enchantments must be settling down now. We'll be able to find it easily, easy being a relative term, of course."

Galene closed her eyes at the small reminder of what she had lost. She knew that Dessie didn't mean to, but she was still a bit mad at her for bringing it up. *And the others are so oblivious*, she thought ruefully.

"Alright. Active volcanoes are the only place that I can think of where fire is dominant but the other Elements are present. Since the enchantments must be only just settling, there should be some disturbance in the nature in that place. I suppose we could check for any volcanic activity in the past ten days."

"Let's make it twenty, just to make sure. Cal, Dhar, you guys get on that." Dessie took charge.

"Hey, guys?" Aura sounded from her alcove. "I just thought of something."

"Yeah?" Galene asked.

"You remember that we're more powerful when were together, right?" At their confirmative nods, she forged ahead. "This applies to our, well, magical conscience. If we try to do a spell together, it is stronger." She paused, hesitating. "My guess is that if we try doing the sensing thing together, we'll probably have a better reach, as well as a better sense of light tremors in the magical and natural balance, so to speak."

Caelus nodded slowly. "That makes sense. But we need to meld our magic for that. How?"

"Well, I found something about that." She lifted the book she had on her lap. "There's a passage in this about that."

Mind Magicks arte a deepe magick. The magick requirest the deepeste truste and bonde between the two participantes. The true connectione art when bothe participantes art able to reache into the soule of the othere. The truste muste be unconditionale, and muste not be forced by either of the participantes on the othere.

"Aura, this is for bonding between two people." Caelus interrupted.

She nodded. "There's a line about Heleanovan bonding: it says that the Elements' heirs are the only ones who can actually bond with more than one person at any point in time."

Everybody considered this. "Its a dangerous magic, 'ra." Caelus broke the silence.

She nodded. "That it is, but its the best way to get this done."

Galene glanced at the others. Dhara looked skeptical, and Caelus and Dessie looked resigned. As for herself…

"I'm in." The others looked at her in surprise. "It's our best shot. We won't know if it will work or not unless we try it. I, for one, trust you all with my life."

There was another pause. "Yes," Caelus said, looking into my eyes. "But would you trust us with someone else's? Melete's, say?"

I hesitated, and looked into the depths of his eyes. "Yes," she said with conviction. "You would protect her till the last of your breath, as I would. She is as much your sister as she is mine."

Caelus masked his surprise quickly, though Galene caught it. She smiled at him, and he nodded. "I'm in."

This time, Dessie asked him, "Do you trust us?"

"With my life."

"With Gale's?" Both Caelus and Galene started.

Trust them with my life? She had, needless to say, never felt so confused. *Why is she asking him that*?

He hesitated, which confused her even more. Then he said, "Yes." The room rang with the strength of his belief.

Quickly, the others too agreed to the bond. The Heleanova agreed to do it the next day, and went to rest.

And through the night, Galene thought about a certain boy with striking blue-green eyes.

CHAPTER 7

The next morning found the Heleanova sitting at the 5 corners of a five point star that they had drawn on a small granite floor in one of the other dimensions. They had agreed that once the merge was over, Galene would direct their search for the Pyrós. In truth, she was feeling a bit nervous about leading the search. If she made one mistake, one slipup… Well, she tried not to think about it.

The five closed their eyes and reached out with their minds to the other Heleanova. Flailing like a small babe in a mother's arms, they reached out to their companions. But that did them no good, until-

The freshest of breezes, the cleanest of winds, the clearest of skies.

Aura? Galene reached tentatively. *Is that you?*

Gale? Came the answering thought.

Together, they tread through the emptiness that was their loneliness, forging bonds that ran deeper than friendship, deeper that water, deeper than blood. They were one.

They searched for the others, until one of them – it was hard to tell whom – brushed against the barest of moistness. Immediately, their senses were flooded with the vastness that was the sea, the swiftness that was the river, the purity that was the spring, the clarity that was the lake, the beauty that was the ocean.

Cal, they said, reaching out to him.

Gale, 'Ra. He joined us.

Quickly, they searched for the other two. They soon felt the calm, the life, the homeliness of the Earth.

Dhar. The four of them searched for the last Helianov, but, unsurprisingly, they found her easily. They felt her Darkness, her Light, her sorrow, her might, her happiness, her life, her Magic. They made it their own, and gave her theirs in exchange.

And so the five Heleanova became one, magic previously unknown, untried, untested, but so powerful that they at once felt at peace.

Let us go, Amiena[1], said Galene, *lest we be too late to find them.*

The other Enver[2] agreed, and so they spread their conscience, searching for the Pyrós. They meditated, and got so engrossed into their task that no one knew how much time had passed.

1 Friend

2 Bonded

Finally, they opened their eyes. Galene blinked. "Wow." The others just nodded. The five could literally see the power, the magic, in each of them. Galene saw in each of them a small amount of the other four's powers, as well as a large amount of their own. The magic wove together, in and out, and spread through the room, and, it seemed, through the world. They stood, mesmerized, as they watched the magic interact with and within the five point star. The true magic, magic of the Elements, was everywhere. They were just fortunate enough to be able to use it. Everyone had it, everything had it – or rather, it had everything. It made everything, created the world, with varying amounts of each.

Aura was the first to come out of the trance. "Let's get started, shall we?"

The others nodded, and grinned. "Let's go!"

The Pyrós was, as they feared, in another universe, another dimension, if you will. Why were they happy, you might ask. Because that dimension was the easiest to reach, and the easiest to get out of, but more importantly, they found a way to find the other weapons.

Galene found that ever since her descriptions, the others had been practically drooling for their weapons. She grinned at the thought of their longing – Caelus had-

Caelus. She shivered. She had no idea – but she did. She had chosen to ignore his signs, just as she ignored her own. *Caelus,* she thought, letting the name roll over her mental tongue. Did she feel – did he truly – oh, it was so confusing.

Caelus. She shivered again, feeling cold. *It won't happen anyway. I am Fire. He is Water. It will never work.*

Somehow, that didn't make her feel better.

"Ready?" Dessie was dressed for a long trip, simple and nothing unexpected. The only exception was a small bag of darts at her waist, with a small tube to blow them out of. Slightly cliché, yes, but she was a devil with them. She could hit a monkey when it was climbing up a tree, and she was falling. And yes, she'd actually tried. She wore a black t-shirt, with black jeans and a black jacket with silver colored simple patterns. Yes, she decided to go all out black.

"Yeah!" Aura was ever the enthusiast. She was the polar opposite of Dessie, going all white, with a crossbow. She could hit a moving target going at 50 miles an hour, when she was going 50 miles an hour in the opposite direction.

Galene was between the two, with a white t-shirt, blue jeans, black boots, and a brown jacket. "Let's hit the road."

"What about us?" The boys climbed down from wherever it was they were. Dhara was wearing a simple t-shirt and jeans, with a lone knife at his waist. "Weapons?" He asked, looking at Galene. She flicked her wrists, calling the knives to her hands. Dhara nodded.

Caelus was wearing simple stuff too, except he had a short sword at his waist. "Let's get going, then."

The five Heleanova stepped closer and held hands, saying one word.

"Celanus[1]."

---

1 Land of fire; volcano

CHAPTER 8

They stepped out, true to its name, onto a land of Fire. They could see fire everywhere, both physically and magically.

"Wow." Caelus said one word – no, made one sound – but that was enough. Galene and Caelus realized that they were still holding hands, and let go immediately, shuffling their feet awkwardly, trying to stand a little away from each other.

"We should stick close," Dhara said, oblivious. The two Heleanova scowled at him, and stepped closer to each other, making the place descend in awkward silence. "Let's go on, shall we?" said Aura in a conversational tone that she used only when she was trying to break the ice.

Galene cleared her throat and nodded. "Yeah." She stepped away from Caelus and started moving north. Then she froze.

"Stop." She whispered, extending her hands. "There's something here – some trap."

Caelus knelt on the ground next to her. "Feels clean to me."

"Exactly," she said, scowling. "Every other bit of the place is positively soaked with magic. Don't you think that that's a bit odd?"

Dhara stepped forward carefully. *Maybe we should search together.* The others nodded quickly, but Galene and Caelus hesitated.

Am I ready to feel that again? To know, that though we want it, we can never get it? Her own thought surprised her. She'd never thought about it, always veered away from completing the thought.

Well, she thought wryly as she nodded her acceptance, *that's what they say: better to have loved and lost than to have never loved at all.*

She vaguely noticed Caelus nod as well, and reached out with her magic, joining her fellow Heleanova.

Shall we? She asked, thinking of going into this together.

Lead on, Gale, came the answer.

Galene took a deep breath, and slowly, painfully slowly, extended their magic over the ground in front of them. No sooner had she done this, they felt a block. Their magic started piling up against this barrier, forming a mix of their magic that was so intense, so powerful, that it was almost impossible to stop.

Withdraw, Galene!

Come out, Gale!

Gale, pull out!

Gale!

The voices sounded as a medley in her head, so strange, loud. She needed quiet, not loudness.

Galene. One voice stood out amongst them all, hot as burning coals. *Come.*

No, Gale! The others sounded again, desperate.

I need to guys. She was quiet, resigned. *It is my weapon, and thus my duty to get it.*

Dhara – who had thus been quiet, she noted with surprise – said, *She is correct. She needs to go on her own. Look.*

The Heleanova glanced at the barrier, and saw that no magic passed through it, except Galene's.

Sorry. "I'm so sorry," she whispered out loud, and withdrew.

"No, Gale!" Caelus yelled, starting towards her. The others held him back. "Wait!"

She shook my head. "I can't." Then, before she could lose her courage, she stepped through the barrier.

Immediately, all noise ceased, and the silence weighed heavily on her. She couldn't feel any of the others, and this bothered her. She hadn't realized just how much she had come to depend on her friends for strength of mind, body and magic. She felt oddly exposed without them to protect her, and she sighed. *I suppose,* she thought, *that it's good that this happened, then. I can learn to be independent* and *get my weapon.*

That jolted her out of her thoughts. She had gotten distracted. "Focus, Galene," she admonished herself. She closed her eyes. Where could it be? She cast her magic in front of her again, gently, slowly, carefully, but the entire area seemed to be devoid of magic. She pursed her lips. Then she summoned her knives to her hands, and slowly stepped forward. Nothing. Another step. Nothing. A third.

Boom. Galene froze.

Boom. She backed down nervously, raising her knives.

Boom.

And then there was a rush of hot air, which was her only warning.

A torrent of Fire, hot enough to turn the stones around her red from proximity, rushed straight at her. She raised her hands, and forced the fire to stop. It fought, as desperate to be free as she was to contain it. Galene knew that she couldn't extinguish it, it was too strong, but she had to try. Slowly, she breathed in, and out. She made the torrent narrower, taming it to one of Aura's little tornadoes – small and playful. It resisted, nearly breaking free of its bonds.

Suddenly, as though granted a new burst of strength, the fire expanded, and Galene fell to her knees. She never let her control waver, though, and brought the fire to its knees with her. The fire seemed to grow, but she never gave up. She couldn't let it hurt her friends, she just couldn't!

"No," she growled. "You will not hurt anyone, least of all my Amiena!"

And the fire dissipated.

Galene started, shocked. Then she narrowed her eyes, and picked up her knives, which she had dropped at the onset of the Firestorm. There was a gentle, warm glow further down the path, if you could call it that. She stepped towards it, never letting her guard down. Suddenly, five women appeared in front of her.

One had ethereal eyes that looked like the depth of the lava itself, and with hair that was red as her own, like the deepest of fires. Her dress was fire, pure, sparkling fire, from hot white to a cooler yellow. Her expression was one of fierce joy, not unlike her own when she saw fire at its best, life-giving and warmth-bringing. Her eyes had the look that made Galene think that she had lived thousands of years, and seen everything there is to be seen.

The second was a woman with eyes that looked like a storm raging first in the sea, then in the desert, then amidst a forest – ever changing, never stopping.

She wore a simple grey dress, but that too seemed to shift, like a tornado had somehow solidified and shaped itself to become this shifting, beautiful fabric.

The third woman had green eyes, brought out by her dark green dress. She had a smile on her face that was pure, unlike so many others that she had seen earlier. She was genuinely happy, and Galene was too.

On the other end was a woman in dark blue, with eyes in the same shade. She was the frozen lake in mid December, when the lights are dark but hope shines bright.

"Between the woods and the frozen lake,

The darkest evening of the year..."[1]

And this was the last woman, dressed in black with black eyes and hair. She was the longest night, the quietest spirit, the calmest life.

"We are the Riella Ranve, the Elements' apparitions, if you will." This was Water.

"We have deemed you worthy of the title of Heleanov fa Pyra, Heir of Fire." Added Fire.

"We give you the gift of the Pyrós, in the hope that you will use it better than we and our parents, the Elements, have used them." Galene's eyes widened when she heard Air's words. They were the Children of the Elements?

---

1 Stopping by the woods on a snowy evening

"These are your powers, to help you in your greatest hour of need." This was Ether.

"Live well, daughter," blessed Earth. The Ranve disappeared, and she looked behind them.

There, floating towards her was the Pyrós.

She had done it.

CHAPTER 9

Caelus was pacing on the floor of the volcano, restless and worried. "What's taking her so long?" He demanded, for, probably, the tenth time in as many minutes.

The others sighed, and Caelus scowled. He knew he shouldn't be taking out his frustration on them, but it was so hard. They didn't seem very worried about Galene at all!

"Caelus," said Dhara in a long suffering voice, "as I have explained for the-"

"Tenth time!" Aura interjected. Caelus scowled at her.

"The barrier is too strong. We will wait for five more minutes, before we attempt to break the barrier and go after Galene."

Caelus scowled even harder. "Five minutes could mean the difference between life and death!" he snapped, scowling.

Despione stepped forward. "We would have felt it if she even scraped her knees. Stop pacing and sit down. You're making my head spin."

Caelus scowled (again) and opened his mouth to retort, but just then, the barrier shattered, and Galene stepped through. Her arms were shaking, like she'd just used a lot of her powers. Her expression was, however, one of pure joy, and she grinned.

Aura, of course, was the first one to recover from her shock. "Galene," she choked out. "What – what are you *wearing*?" she squealed, making the rest of the Heleanova wince.

Galene blinked and looked down. Then she blinked once. Twice. Thrice. "Wow." The rest of them just nodded. She was wearing a dress made of fire, first blue, then white, then yellow, then red – ever shifting. Galene, surprisingly, broke out of her reverie quickly, making him suspect that she had seen the dress before. *But where?* He thought.

At her waist, there was a red belt, with a golden buckle. Hanging from it was a red sheath, with the dagger inside it. "Ready?" Galene asked, grinning. The others nodded. She took a deep breath, and drew it.

It was exactly like how Galene had described it, like a blade with flames dancing on it - no, a blade made of flames, deadly and yet, reassuring. For Caelus, it was a promise, a promise that said that it was possible, that they could, they would, stay together. Forever.

Galene sheathed her blade, and closed her eyes. Immediately, the dress shifted into one more suited for travel. She wore an orange tunic with brown pants and boots. The Pyrós was at her waist, and Caelus had a sneaking suspicion that she had her daggers up her sleeves.

She cleared her throat. "Kÿma next, then?"

Caelus narrowed his eyes. "You, miss, are going to rest. Your arms are shaking, a clear sign of magical exhaustion, indicating that you used your Riella's inheritance, which means you need to rest. We will call it a day, and leave for wherever the Kÿma is tomorrow."

The other Heleanova nodded, and Galene sighed. "I didn't think anyone would notice. I'm fine."

Caelus snorted. "Right. You are exhausted, you used your Riella's inheritance, but of course, you're fine."

Galene pursed her lips, and then nodded. "Fine."

Caelus pointed to a spot behind Galene. "Thryst.[1]"

A tent sprung up, and he nodded at Galene. "Get in, and *rest*."

1 Tent

Galene sighed. "Yes, sir." She said sarcastically, and then went in. Caelus looked at Aura, and she nodded. "Thanks," he said, and summoned another tent for Dhara and himself.

"Shall we?" He asked, grinning at Dhara.

The latter rolled his eyes. "Good night, Cal."

Chapter 10

"Good morning, boys!" Aura stuck her head into their tent. "It's a bright sunny day, and we're about to go on an adventure! Would you care to join us?"

"Bleargh."

"Am I right in assuming, Caelus, that you want five more minutes?"

Grunt.

"Well, then, Galene is threatening to leave without you."

"What!" Caelus sat up, shocked.

Aura raised her eyebrows, amused. "That woke you up. And yes, you heard me right. So get up!" She started pulling out, but she paused. "And take a bath! You smell."

The boys started spluttering, and heard all three of the girls laughing. "Not funny," called Caelus, red.

"Of course not," came the sarcastic reply.

Fifteen minutes later, the boys walked out of the tent in travelling clothes. "Not one word," warned Galene. She was wearing her tunic and breeches, and seemed rather self conscious.

"Why not?" Asked Caelus. "You look good. Not that," he added quickly, "you don't usually, just that, well – never mind." He finished inelegantly, the back of his neck heating up. Galene was red too, but she smiled and nodded.

"Thanks. Shall we search?" She seemed eager to do it. Probably to get it over with.

Caelus nodded. "Sure."

The five Heleanova sat, and extended their conscience towards each other. This time, the joining was faster, since each of them knew how the others felt.

Galene? Called Caelus. *Will you lead?*

You and I. She replied. *We need to look for the Kÿma, after all.*

Alright, thought Caelus. They extended their conscience further, leading the other Heleanova on the search.

Soon, they felt the slight ripple that marked the transition between two worlds. The moment they entered the neighboring world, Caelus relaxed. They were home, and they were underwater. *My personal heaven.*

Caelus! Galene sounded panicked.

Yeah?

I'm underwater! I'm Fire! Fire is not meant to be under water! Get me out*!* Galene was floundering.

Calm down.

Calm down! She sounded really panicked now. *You expect me to* calm down?

Galene! Caelus shouted mentally. Galene froze, and calmed down. She appeared to take a deep breath, and she reached towards Caelus.

And he touched fire for the first time.

That was Galene – a torrent of the wildest, fiercest colors, dancing together with a hypnotizing beauty. She was the glowing ember of a fireplace, the dark flames of the firestorm, the pale light of the stars, the bright life of the sun – she had them all. She was fire – pure, powerful fire.

You've been holding out on us, Caelus said mildly.

No, Galene replied. *Some of my power got unlocked in the cavern. Not all, but some. I wasn't sure if I could contain it. I didn't want to hurt you.* There was a pause. *Any of you.*

Caelus nodded, though he wasn't sure if Galene saw it. *Let's go, then.*

They continued in their search, venturing deeper and deeper into the ocean, into depths not many had gone into before. Galene's flames spread, covering the area, searching for the weapon. Caelus' water flowed close behind, quenching fires that would have otherwise spread. Aura, Dhara and Despione each searched in nooks and corners that the others might have missed in their broad search. But it was all for naught.

Finally, when they were on the verge of giving up, Caelus felt a glimmer of magic that was not their own. He turned to it, and immediately turned away. *Galene?* He called. *I think I found it, but it's too bright.*

Galene turned to the place he indicated. *Yes,* she said. *It's there.*

They came out of the bond, blinking as they adjusted to the new light. Caelus got up, and stretched. "Oh, God," he moaned. "I'm so *stiff.*"

Galene rose. "I'm not. Not really." And she wasn't. Caelus looked at her, and she seemed to move with the same ease with which she always did. "Shall we?" Galene asked, eyebrows raised.

"Yeah." Caelus responded, nodding. He reached into the tent and grabbed his bag, nodding at Dhara. "Get your stuff. I'll shrink the tent or something."

Dhara stuck his hand inside and pulled his bag out. "Vano."[1] Dhara said, pointing at the tent. It disappeared. He turned to the girls. "You got everything out?" He asked.

In response, Aura grinned and said, "Vano."

1 Disappear, Vanish

Dhara pursed his lips. "All it would have taken was a simple 'yes'," he said.

Aura laughed. "I know, but where's the fun in that?"

"Ready?" Galene asked, cutting off whatever retort Dhara had ready.

The others nodded, and reached out. The Heleanova put their hand on top of one another, looking at each other. "Avar fa Hedro."[1]

There was a swirl of water, coming from the four universes, four different, vivid shades that could only come from the purest seas, oceans, and rivers.

The five appeared at the bottom of a sandy ocean. The ocean was oddly clear, with a few fish darting about here and there. Caelus looked up, and his eyes widened. "The Arctic Grayling! Guys, did you see that?" His voice echoed oddly around the ocean. "Guys?" He turned around to face the others.

Galene extended her hand towards him. She appeared to be holding her breath.

"You want me to hold your hand?" Caelus asked. Galene nodded. Caelus took it, and she gasped.

"We can't breath. This isn't our Element." She bit out. "Get the others," she snapped, doubling over, taking deep breaths. Caelus extended his hand towards the others, and they grabbed it, and let out a breath.

1 Home of Water

"We need a way to breath without holding your hand," said Dhara once he'd recovered sufficiently.

"I can't believe we overlooked this, what with all our plans!" Galene looked supremely annoyed.

"Cal," started Aura, "maybe you and I can create an air bubble or something. I can renew the oxygen, and you can keep it from popping."

Caelus nodded, and closed his eyes. A moment later, a huge bubble appeared around them Aura focused, and the air became fresh.

Come forward, Caelus fa Hedro, Galene fa Pyra.

Caelus of Water.

Galene of Fire.

Galene bit her lips, and clenched her fists. Caelus knew why. That was how her grandfather addressed them initially, when they were still accepting their inheritance. Galene had protested the most. *You say it like we belong to the Element. How can you expect us to accept that we aren't our own, that we must always do what they want us to, that we can't ever, truly, be free?*

Mr. Alwood had replied, *You* are *free. You just don't know it yet.*

The Heleanova hadn't understood it then, and they still couldn't. But with time, maybe, just maybe, they might.

"Go ahead, Galene, Caelus." Dhara told them, jerking his elbow towards where they had estimated the weapon was.

They started moving away, when Aura shouted, "Wait!" They started, and turned towards her. "I can't do this thing long range."

Galene blinked. "Let me get this straight. You can create huge, whopping storms miles away, but you can't renew oxygen a few meters away?" Galene questioned incredulously.

Aura blushed. "I can't, alright? I've tried, but it doesn't work. I can't do that sort of fine control."

"So what do we do?" Asked Galene.

Aura grinned. "You have to hold his hand." They both extended their hands towards each other, trying (and failing) to look like it didn't matter.

"Let's go," said Galene shortly.

"Alright!" Caelus grinned enthusiastically, and the two started waking away, and soon disappeared into the murky blackness that was the deep sea.

CHAPTER 11

"... And then they disappeared, and I saw the Pyrós." Galene told Caelus. She was telling him what had happened in the cavern in the volcano.

Caelus blinked. "The *daughters* of the Elements?" He demanded.

Galene smacked the back of his head with her free hand. "For the tenth time, yes!"

He shook his head. "Wow."

Galene rolled her eyes. Then she froze. "Do you feel something?"

Caelus nodded slowly. "I can't put my finger on it. It's shifting so fast!"

Galene turned so that she stood back to back with Caelus. They searched the waters, sharing what they saw through the bond. They couldn't see anything, but they couldn't shake off the feeling that they were being watched. Finally, Galene shook her head. "Let's keep walking," she said softly, her eyes still scanning the water.

They kept walking, but they were more vigilant than before. Caelus pulled out his sword, holding it up so he would be ready no matter what. Galene pulled out the Pyrós. Suddenly, there was a loud hiss, and a spurt of fire flew from the Pyros. The fire hit a barrier in front of them, and sputtered out. The barrier rippled, and then calmed. If they didn't know that it was there, they probably wouldn't have noticed it. "Cal?" said Galene softly.

Caelus raised his hand. A sea green bolt of energy shot out of his palm, striking the barrier. The barrier shuddered, and solidified. The next moment, Caelus was on his knees, clutching Galene's arm tightly. His magic-

"Caelus!" shouted Galene, kneeling in front if him. "What's wrong?"

Caelus gasped. "It's leeching off my energy," he wheezed. "I can't stop it."

Galene grabbed Caelus' chin. "Cal, look at me." He didn't respond. "Caelus." He blinked, and looked into her eyes. "It must be like the firestorm in the cavern. You can stop it. I know you can. Come on, Cal. break free. Cut the bond. You are strong enough for this."

Slowly, her words came through the haze of pain that surrounded him. He extended his arm weakly and closed his eyes. He caught hold of the next stream of his power that was flowing away. He redirected it towards himself, forcing the other magic to let go. He drew the power back into himself. *My friends need me,* he thought. *Galene needs me.* He gasped and opened his eyes.

And met the blue-rimmed golden eyes of Galene.

Wait, blue-rimmed?

"What happened to your eyes?" He demanded.

"I could ask you the same thing," she retorted. "I think you accidentally transferred some of your power to me when you were drawing it back. You didn't give it a specific place to go, so some of it pooled into me too. I had to give you some of mine as well. So now you have gold-rimmed blue eyes, and I, presumably, have Blue-rimmed gold eyes." Caelus nodded, speechless. "Get up. We need to continue, before the others send a search party for us." Caelus nodded and got up.

And gasped.

Galene whirled around, snapping into a defensive position. Then she straightened, putting the Pyrós into the sheath. "Don't scare me like that," she rebuked.

Caelus opened and closed his mouth. "Oh my God." He finally said, staring.

"Riella Ranve," corrected Galene, grinning.

And so they were. Fire, Air, Water, Ether, Earth – they were living proof that things could work out, that they could stay together, and keep peace. Caelus felt himself relaxing at the thought.

Earth's smile widened, like she knew what he had thought. "Welcome, Caelus fa Hedro. And well met, Galene fa Pyra."

"Well met, Riella Ranve," said Galene, smiling. "Well met indeed."

"You have proven yourself strong enough to wield the Kÿma, young Helianov." Water smiled, looking down at Caelus kindly.

Caelus blinked. "But I couldn't stop the barrier from sapping my inheritance. How can I be powerful enough?"

Fire smiled. "Remember one thing, young Heleanova. Your power defines you. Not," she raised her hand, preempting Caelus' response, "the amount you have, as many have come to believe. You are defined by its purity, its use. If you use it without regard of the consequences, it will be chaotic. *You* will be chaotic. But you are not, and hence you are worthy."

Caelus throat clogged up. "Thank you," he said quietly, trying to convey his entire feelings through those two words.

Ether nodded. "Both Hedro and the Kÿma have chosen you. You are truly worthy."

"Take your weapon, Helianov, and keep yourself and your heart pure." They disappeared at Air's words, and behind them floated the Kÿma.

Caelus walked towards it slowly, staring at it. "It truly is real," he said. "I thought, sometimes, that maybe this was just a dream, but it isn't. It's the truth." He reached out and grasped the blade, feeling the way it rested on his palm. "It's beautiful," he said, mesmerized by the way the blade seemed to be made of water, beautiful, pure, shifting, solid, whole. He slowly buckled the belt onto his jeans, and blinked.

"Whoa." He was wearing a tunic and pants that seemed to be the deepest of the deep lakes in winter. Not that color, but the actual lake. Caelus blinked, and shook his head. "I can't wear this," he said, looking up at Galene.

"Change it. Think about what you want to wear, and it will change."

Travel-wear, he thought, feeling a little foolish. However, his fear was unfounded, as it immediately changed into an ordinary white tunic and brown pants, with the Kÿma on one side of his waist, and his other sword on the other. Caelus looked up at Galene's eyes, thinking.

She looks just the same, he thought, *and yet so different. I should tell her – but she knows – but-*

His thoughts were interrupted by a scream from the depths of the ocean.

Their eyes met. “Aura!” They shouted simultaneously, running towards where they had left their friends.

Chapter 12

Caelus ran as fast as he could, his heart thudding in his chest. *Why did we leave them? They were limited with what they could do, what with them being underwater.* He ran faster. Galene ran right next to him, Pyrós in hand. Caelus himself had the Kÿma in his hand. Finally, they reached the spot they left the other Heleanova.

"Split!" Yelled Galene, jumping to the right. Caelus jumped to the left, using his power over water to hurl him further.

"What *is* that thing?" Caelus demanded, keeping his eyes on the creature.

Apparently, that thing didn't like being called that thing, and turned to him. Caelus raised the Kÿma warily. "Uh, Galene?" Caelus started backing up.

One moment. I'm thinking. Galene told him through the bond.

Think fast! Retorted Caelus, feeling more than a bit panicky.

Galene snapped her fingers. "Dellione!" She said, eyes widening. "She was hurled into the ocean after Fire and Water failed to control her!"

At those words, the she-lion roared and turned to Galene. Fire sprouted from its maw, engulfing Galene in a cage of fire.

"Galene!" shouted Caelus moving forward.

The fire cleared, and Galene stood, unscathed. "You're going to have to do better than that, kitty!" She yelled, running forward with the Pyrós in hand. She pulled her hand back, and leapt up onto the lioness.

"How was she defeated?" Caelus asked, waving the Kÿma, distracting the creature.

"Fire and Water worked together, repeatedly beating her down until she stayed down."

Caelus nodded. "Fire and Water. We can do that. Let's go!" He ran at the lion, but instead of jumping up, like Galene had, he slid down, cutting her underbelly. He rolled and got back to his feet.

And was promptly knocked down again.

"Gale!" He yelled, glaring at her. "Next time, not on me, OK?"

"Hopefully," Galene got up, "there won't be a next time." She glanced at him. *You go left, I go right,* she told him through the link.

Alright. He went to the right, and she went to the left. Then they leapt to the other side, and the poor lioness got confused. They jumped in, but they were pushed back by her paws. She roared again, this time leaping at Galene. She rolled back, dodging the first swipe, then the next, and the next. *Cal!* She screamed through the bond.

"Hey, Leo!" he yelled, tossing a small rock next to him onto her.

Dellione turned, roaring. She bounded towards him, and Galene jumped onto her back again. While Galene tried desperately to hang on, she told Caelus her plan.

I think Fire and Water actually worked together, like using both their powers to the extent where neither knew who did what. I think, here her tone became wry, *we'll have no trouble doing that.*

Caelus nodded his agreement, and shouted, "NOW!"

They both unleashed torrents of fire and water, with Galene leaping off Dellione's back. When they finally stopped their powers, they looked up. The lioness was badly burned, but was healing fast. She roared, and sent a torrent of fire back at Caelus.

"Caelus!" screamed Galene, running towards him.

She was too slow.

He braced himself for the heat, but it didn't burn. Instead of biting like a sworn enemy, it embraced him like a long lost friend. *We're still separate,* he told Galene through the bond.

Cal? Galene asked, confused.

Yes. And no, you are not going mad. Unless I am as well.

Not much reassurance.

Ha ha. Very funny.

I transferred some of my powers to you, and you to me. That's how you can breath, and how I'm not getting burnt.

There was a pause in their conversation. *Now.* Caelus said with conviction.

Immediately, he leapt out of the fiery embrace, and threw some balls of energy at her. First it was water, then fire, then a combination of both, until, like Galene said, they could no longer tell who did what.

Finally, after an eternity, Dellione stopped healing, and the two Heleanova stepped forward, raising their weapons.

"Together?" asked Galene.

"Of course," replied Caelus.

And they brought their weapons down, defeating the Dellione.

CHAPTER 13

"Aura!" called Galene. They'd been looking for them for the past half hour, and were beginning to get worried. "Dessie!"

"Dhar!" yelled Caelus, walking in the opposite direction. "Dhara!"

Finally, Galene shook her head. "Despione Griffon, I swear, if you don't come out right now, I burn down your tent, with the photos in them!" Caelus looked at Galene, curious.

"Oh, didn't you know?" laughed Galene, her eyes sparkling. *Oh, God, she looks so good like that,* he thought. Then he mentally slapped himself. *Focus,* he scolded himself.

"She sleeps with these photos under her pillow. I got curious one day, and looked at them. They were-"

She didn't finish her sentence as she was interrupted by a ball of darkness. "Oi!" yelled Galene indignantly. "If you didn't want me to say, you could've just said so, instead of chucking that at me!"

Dessie stepped out, her palms covered with Ethereal power. "How do I know that you really are who you say you are?"

"First of all," started Caelus, only to be interrupted by Galene.

"What will it take to convince you?"

"More than your eyes, that's for sure."

Galene rolled her eyes. "We came across a barrier that drained his powers. He pulled it back, but, of course, he was clumsy. I got some of his powers, and it ended up as an exchange. Hence," she gestured towards Caelus, "the result."

"Who're you calling clumsy?" Caelus demanded, annoyed.

"You," said Galene, rolling her eyes again.

"I'm not clumsy!"

"Are too!"

"Are not!"

"Are too!"

"Are not!"

"Are too!"

"Are not!"

"Are too!"

"Are not!"

"Are-"

"Well," Dessie interrupted. "You've certainly convinced me. No one could possibly pseudo-flirt like you did."

"We were not flirting!" snapped Galene and Caelus. *Though I wish we were,* thought Caelus privately.

I heard that! snapped Galene.

Caelus winced. Maybe not so privately.

Galene glared at him and turned to the others, and started a conversation.

And then Dhara, being the fool he was, decided to open his mouth at that moment.

Chapter 14

Different.

That was an understatement.

Caelus and Galene had changed so much that it was nigh impossible to comprehend. And she wasn't talking about their eyes either. Sure, they somehow managed to accomplish the impossible and change them within the small time they'd been separated – and it couldn't have been that long, now, could it? – with their eyes so much more striking and their faces much more set – there was no other word for it. Galene's eyes were earlier striking gems of gold, glittering with their ardor, but now, it was a dance between topaz and sapphire, flashing, here and there, a beautiful pattern for those who didn't get distracted by the enticing frolic in those windows of the soul. And Caelus eyes, earlier glittering, green gems, now seemed to be duet between the green elegance of emerald and the golden dauntlessness of yellow sapphire – so rare, so beautiful, so lovely, that one couldn't help but fall into them.

But no, she wasn't talking about that.

She was talking about their demeanor, their newfound confidence, their closeness. They weren't just together, not just bonded – they all were – but this was more. This closeness, this familiarity, seemed more than the other Heleanova – herself included – could understand.

And she couldn't help but feel jealous.

Of course, she was happy for them, but there was some part of her that couldn't just let go, let go of her first –

No, she wouldn't say it. It was better to forget about it, drown it in small smiles and laughs and her usual grace. She was happy for her friend, her sister, but sometimes, it was just so hard to let go, and now she knew. She just hoped that no one ever found out. But they had changed, and so must she.

Become different.

"Who next, Gale?" A day ago, Galene would have snapped at Caelus, telling him to *stop calling me by that ridiculous thing you call a nickname!* As it was, she just raised her eyebrows and smiled.

"Well," she grinned. "I guess, Astrapí?"

Aura pulled a smile on her face. "Awesome!" she cheered. "Let's ride the wind, people!"

"Great. Let's go, shall we?" Galene started getting up, only to be pulled down by Caelus.

"Gale, I know you're eager, but maybe we could rest for a while?"

Her face darkened. "You don't get them?" she demanded, scowling.

"What?" he asked.

Galene shook her head. "I- never mind." She sighed. "We'll start tomorrow right after we grab a bite to eat, alright?"

"Galene, what were you talking about?"

"It's nothing, alright?" She growled, her eyes dancing with fire and – was that a storm? Before Aura could continue that train of thought, Dhara cut in.

"Gale?"

"Never. Mind." She snapped, glaring at him. *If looks could kill,* Aura thought wryly, *we'd all be dead ten times over.*

"Galene, Cal's right," Aura said gently. "Besides," she added with a teasing grin. "I'm tired, superhuman."

"Well, Gale?" asked Dessie. Aura started. Dessie had been so quiet she'd nearly forgotten about her. *True to her element,* thought Aura.

"Alright." Galene finally agreed, sighing her displeasure.

"But first," Dhara interjected, frowning. "Explain."

Galene coolly raised an eyebrow. "Pardon?"

Uh oh, Aura thought. *Alert! Annoyed Helianov!*

"What happened when we separated?" pressed Dhara, ignoring the signs. "You owe us an explanation."

Caelus, Dessie and Aura exchanged looks. *Major uh oh,* Aura thought, subtly putting up shields.

And not a moment too soon.

Galene's power flared, and she glared at Dhara. "Let's get something straight, Helianov Dhara. I don't owe you anything, explanation or otherwise. If you're curious, then *ask*. Don't *demand*. Knowing is not your right, and you certainly can't demand it. If we want to, or feel the need to answer your questions, then you'll get your answer. Otherwise, you might just find yourself on the wrong side of something powerful, and you'll regret it."

Dhara's eyes narrowed. "Is that a threat?"

"No," said Galene, her smile having a bitter edge. "It's a certainty."

And with that, she ducked into her tent.

"Good Morning!" Aura peeked into the girl's tent after she'd gotten ready.

"Go back to sleep, 'Ra," mumbled Dessie, turning over.

"Get up, Dessie." Galene entered the tent, wearing her tunic, breeches, with her knives up her sleeves, and the Pyrós at her waist, her hair tied in a ponytail. "We need to get moving."

"Why?" grumbled Dessie, still talking to the pillow. "Can't we sleep for a few more minutes?"

"No."

"Why not?" Galene pierced her with a glare, and Dessie rolled off her makeshift bed. "Gimme five minutes," she said, blinking the sleep out of her eyes. "I'll be ready."

"You'd better be." With one last look, she left.

There was a pause. "She's changed." Dessie looked out at where Galene had stood.

"Yeah." Pause. "You'd best get to it."

"Yeah."

And with that, Aura left.

"Ready?" Caelus asked. He'd changed as much as Galene had, and that was saying something.

Aura took a deep breath. She knew where to go. *"Aether*[1]*."*

1 Upper air

And all was calm.

The Heleanova looked around, standing back to back.

"Oh." Aura started.

"My." Dessie enunciated.

"God!" they finished together.

"That, my dear friends," Galene stated, her eyes sparkling with the fervor that came only with the rush of adrenaline during an adventure, "is an understatement."

The Heleanova were standing in the middle of a raging cyclone that, if Aura's readings were correct, extended at least a few thousand kilometers across, with wind speeds breaking all earthly records. And yet, the eye of the cyclone was a tall, narrow cone of calm and silence, with none of the harsh winds coming within.

"Feel anything?" Caelus asked Galene.

She shook her head. "I need to identify the pattern behind this thing."

Aura raised her eyes. "It's an outward spiral, of course. One false step, and you're out of here the hard way."

"Yes," said Galene nodding. "But that's the surface pattern. The enchantment used to hide the Astrapí has several layers, sometimes overlapping, sometimes so far apart that nothing seems to connect them but the thinnest of fibers. A complex web of the

Elements, intricate layers that can be broken by the most delicate cares, the most fleeting touch. A fabric where even one knot, when misplaced, destroys the entire work."

She breathed out, extending her arms, feeling with her magic the deeper patterns that shrouded the Astrapí. Aura closed here eyes, extending herself towards the Pÿra Helianov.

We need to look for any small changes in the story your predecessor created – small unexpected happenings in the way it's been written. Galene instructed her.

No, said Aura, disagreeing. *That's what you won't find.*

What do you mean? Caelus questioned. Aura started. She didn't know he was there.

It's what I'd do. Give them what they expect when they least expect it. A double bluff, in a way. The truth, hidden in what they think is a lie. I'd hide it where the story proceeded exactly the way I expected it to be. That predictable pattern is what one would least expect from Air, this effectively ensuring that no one could find it except his Helianov.

A good plan, said Galene. *Lead on, Aura.*

Follow me, people!

She gently forged forward, sending a zephyr ahead of her, following the path traced by the dancing ripples disturbed by her winds.

Soon, she pulled out of the pattern, telling the other Heleanova her findings. "The Astrapí," she bit her lips in frustration. "It's at the bottom of this thing. It's at the foot of the cyclone."

Chapter 15

"Let's go, shall we?" Asked Galene calmly, like she was calling them to the supermarket.

Aura stared. "I just told you that the Astrapí is at the bottom of a super massive cyclone, and you're saying, 'Let's go'?" she demanded, incredulous.

Galene shrugged. "I trust you."

Aura gaped. "'The fate of all the Heleanova is on your shoulders, but no pressure. I trust you.' Way to reassure and pressurize at the same time, Gale."

Galene grinned. "You have your powers under control."

"If it helps," Caelus added, smiling mischievously, "I trust you too."

Aura pursed her lips. "Yes and no, Caelus, yes and no." She looked down, trying to figure out the best way of getting down. Suddenly, she yelled out in frustration.

"What's wrong, 'Ra?" Galene asked gently.

Aura gulped. "I know it's crazy, but it's the only way. The direct way won't work,"

"Aura." Galene tried.

"There are wards, and-"

"Aura." Galene tried again.

"There's no way to get out of this thing, and-"

"Aura!" she yelled.

"What!"

"Tell us," she said gently.

Aura sighed. "We need to step into the storm. Become part of it. Jump-"

"We get it," Galene interrupted. "I thought that might be the case."

There was dead silence, except for the storm. "Pardon me," said Aura, finally, the calm before the storm. "Correct me if I'm wrong, but I thought you said that you thought we might need to join the storm."

"Not exactly that," she said, "But I thought it might be something to test your power. I had the firestorm, Caelus had the ward, you have the storm."

Aura slumped and buried her head in her hands. "I don't know if I can do it." She mumbled through her hands.

Galene knelt next to her. "You can. You've managed to create a storm inside the eye of a cyclone to hold us, and you're holding it. I know you can do this." Aura hesitated, unsure.

"You can do this," said Caelus, calmly, seriously. "We all know that."

Aura straightened and squared her shoulders. "I can do this," she said resolutely. "Let's go."

She started moving, pulling small tendrils of the storm towards them, one for each of them. The Heleanova stepped on them, and they moved back into the storm.

Suddenly, something went wrong. "Aura!" Dhara yelled, seemingly hanging onto Aura's first storm. Dessie was next to him, desperately trying to pull them up. "Help!"

Aura sent a bolt of grey energy at them, heart thudding. "Dhar! Dess!"

The storm steadied, and Dhara and Dessie clambered on. "We're OK!" He yelled. "Can you maintain this over long distances?"

Aura grinned. "Even better!"

She concentrated on her power, taking out two beads of it and stringing it onto a small sliver of icy winds, which solidified into bracelets and appeared on their hands. "That'll keep you up for at least an entire day," she told them, and then nodded to the other two. Together, they stepped into the cyclone.

Aura flew downwards, Galene and Caelus right behind her. She was having a hard time keeping the winds from ripping Galene apart, convincing them she was a friend. They were not quite as antagonized by Caelus, but the animosity was still there. They were more focused on Galene, but that didn't mean it was easier keeping the winds away from Caelus. One strand of this power could rip apart a mountain. This wasn't true for most cyclones, but with this magnitude, and the power that her predecessor infused in it, the strength was overwhelming.

It was liberating.

After all those weeks of having to hold back, of keeping her power tightly reigned, she could finally be free. Wind. Calming, on occasions. But a deadly force, which many people overlook. Even a small breeze could push something off the edge, and a strong gust had power to do much more. Intoxicating, often malignant, it was a force to be reckoned with. And the thing is, no one knew. She had to keep down. She couldn't be free.

But now she was.

She laughed fiercely, shooting down, taking the other two down with her, slowing down after a few seconds. Her eyes met Galene's, and they both shared a grin. *It's good to be free,* Galene told her through the bond, *isn't it?*

Aura smiled wryly. *Yeah. They don't know…*

Galene returned the expression. *And they don't know Fire.*

They don't know any of the Elements, said Caelus, smiling at the girls.

And their eyes met.

Galene took a breath. *I…understand.* It seemed almost an age ago, that Mr. Alwood had told them that they were free. And now, here, they understood. They were truly *free*.

And the storm dissipated.

"Welcome, Aura fa Vrar, Caelus fa Hedra, Galene fa Pyra." Fire's eyes sparkled much like Galene's.

Aura gaped. "Well met, Riella Ranve." Caelus said, smirking at Aura's stunned expression. Galene nodded in agreement.

"Um, hi?" was Aura's eloquent response. She mentally smacked herself for such a reaction. *Wake up! Say something* sensible*!*

Water smiled and nodded. "Knowing is different from understanding, Aura fa Vrar, and you have understood the difference."

"As my father's heir, you are most certainly worthy, Aura." Air smiled.

Earth looked at her warmly. "Just remember, young one, never lose hope. Sometimes, it's the only thing we have left."

Aura's throat constricted. *She knows! Sheknowssheknowssheknows!*

Ether cut off Aura's hyperventilation. "Claim the Astrapí, young Helianov."

"We wish you luck."

With that, they disappeared.

Aura slowly stepped forward, towards the Astrapí. She picked up the bow, stringing it with the ease of practice. *It feels…right,* she thought, drawing the string and testing it. *Perfect.*

She picked up the quiver, staring at the star sapphires at the bottom, looking eerily like a storm. Pulling out an arrow, she smiled. *Perfect,* she thought again. It seemed to be a true breeze, and would always fly true. *Astrapí.* She unstrung the bow, and slung the quiver over her shoulder. As she looked down-

"What am I wearing!" She yelled, staring. It looked rather similar to what Air was wearing.

Galene shrugged. "You remember what I was wearing. Just think, travel clothes, and it'll change."

Aura did that, and it changed. *Thank god.* Something less…screaming.

She was wearing a grayish-white tunic, with brown breeches and boots. Her tunic looked rather like a snowstorm, but that couldn't be helped.

"Let's go?" She asked, turning to the others.

Galene nodded. Aura looked up, and called the storm on which the others were standing down. She herself shot up, taking Galene and Caelus with her.

They hit the storm, and the world disappeared.

Chapter 16

"Where did you take us, Aura?" demanded Galene, doubled over after the drop. Oddly, only Galene and Dhara were feeling nauseous. He blinked, clearing his head.

Aura smiled. "Look around."

"Is that?" Galene questioned, drinking in her surroundings. Aura nodded. Galene turned to her, tears in her eyes. "Thank you." She said, hugging her fiercely. Then she ran off, sprinting towards-

"Mr. Alwood's study?!" demanded Dhara, just recognising the place. Aura nodded, rolling her eyes. Dhara tilted his head, confused. "What about Melete?"

Aura was silent for a moment. "She'll be there."

"Ah." Dhara closed his eyes.

"Hileum." Caelus said suddenly, turning their clothes black.

Dhara turned and glared. "What?"

Caelus' eyes were serious. "Mourning."

Dhara turned away, heart clenched. *I should've realized.*

Caelus left, gone to give Galene company, and presumably to warn her about Melete.

Dhara nodded to the others, and left to prepare the guest room for the boys.

And they slept through the night.

Dhara woke up the next day confused. Where was he? The previous day's events came to him in a rush, and he relaxed. *Galene's place.* He climbed out of the bed, and got ready to move again. Then he froze. "Caelus?"

He wasn't there.

He washed his face, neatened his clothes with magic, and went towards Mr. Alwood's study. "Cal?" He called.

"So you've brought everybody with you. Why ever not?" Melete's voice rang through the hall. Dhara ran towards the source, the study. Everybody was there, and Dhara joined the group of three standing behind the elder sister.

"I had to finish something important, Mel-"

"Don't call me that. And nothing's more important than family, and you chose to rip it apart."

"Grandfather told me to do this! I couldn't just leave it be!"

Melete narrowed her eyes. "You never cared about grandfather's wishes. You hated-"

"Don't," Galene said, holding her hand up. "You don't know." Her eyes glistened with unshed tears. "I loved him. After mum and dad," here her voice broke, "you and him – you were all I had left. He was strong when I was weak, he was soft when I was loud, he was calm when I was fire – he was everything. He protected me – us. You more than me, and that won him my respect and love forever."

Melete shook her head, lips curling. "If you loved him, then why-"

"Galene Alwood?" came a voice from the hallway.

"Here!" called Melete, stepping back towards the door. The Heleanova tensed, looking at who came in.

"Inspector Draven?" asked Galene, incredulous, "What're you doing here?"

"Miss Alwood, you have been called in for questioning in the matter of the murder of your grandfather."

There was a stunned silence. "Murder." Galene's voice was rough, displaying, for the first time, her emotion. Draven nodded. Galene turned to Aura, eyes wide. "That's how he knew." She said softly, her breath shallow. "He knew and didn't tell me. He knew I'd be distracted, wouldn't concentrate on his task. He knew…"

And she began to cry in earnest.

She cried for her father, her mother, her grandfather, everything she hadn't mourned for, everything she'd been strong for, everything she'd kept in. She let it all out.

It was oddly calming to watch.

Finally, she controlled herself, and she turned to Melete. "How?" She asked, her voice cracking like a dying fire, her eyes smoldering with her sorrow.

"Poison." said a new voice from the shadows.

"Officer Elethia." Galene's voice could have burnt wet wood.

"Miss Alwood."

"What makes you sure?"

Tell her, Dhara sent to her. *About us.*

Galene was silent. *Very well.* She finally said.

"My magic." Elethia smiled, baring her teeth like a snake exposes its fangs. "I'm a mage."

Galene raised an eyebrow, somehow looking immaculate even after letting everything out. "You don't have magic."

Draven raised his eyebrows. "We've seen it."

Galene smiled. "Without my grandfather at least ten meters in the vicinity?" Without waiting for an answer. "He owed her something, and she wanted to go up in your ranks. He did the magic. She was a prop."

"And how do you know?" He questioned, tilting his head.

"Only Heleanova, Heirs of the Elements, have magic." She grinned, her eyes looking much like wildfire.

"Again, you know this, how?"

"We are Heleanova."

There was a stunned silence.

Elethia broke it. "Prove it."

Galene's smile was positively feral. "With pleasure."

She gestured towards Aura, who stepped forward. "I am Aura fa Vrar, rider of the winds, wielder of the Astrapí, Vrarora by the Element's gift to his first Heir, she of the storm. I am the true Heir of Air." She raised a storm, which became a beautiful orb and went to the center of the room, spinning over a symbol which none of them had seen there before, the Lenaulan letter V:

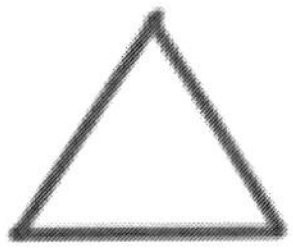

Dhara stepped forward next. He'd been looking forward to this. "I am Dhara fa Finthé, of the gems, of the dirt," here he smiled, like it was a joke only he knew, "of the mud, of the Earth, Finthspíez and wielder of the Gis by my inheritance. I am the true Heir of Earth." He sent a small earthen sphere that seemed to pulse with his power. It flew over the Lenaulan letter F:

Despione came up. "I am Despione fa Ethella, the Mystery and Magic, the Dark and the light, the sky and space, the truth and the lie, the Ethelova, the wielder of the Caelum. I am the true heir of Ether." She sent a ball of darkness towards the other symbols, stopping over the Lenaulan symbol E:

Caelus stepped forward, chin up. "I am Caelus fa Hedro, of the sea, of the ocean, of the river, of the stream, of the lake, of the pond, Hedravista by the will of Hedro, wielder of the Kÿma. I am the true heir of Water." He sent a globe of water towards his Lenaulan symbol, the letter H:

Finally, Galene stepped up. Dhara grinned internally. *Any time now.*

"I am Galene fa Pyra, the firestorm, the heat, the coal, the wildfire, the strength, the passion, the burn, the pyre. I am Pyropathos, from the gift of my predecessor and from our ruler, and wielder of the Pyrós by right. I am the true heir of Fire." She paused to shoot a fireball towards the center, above the symbol P:

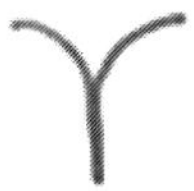

Then, all the Heleanova stepped forward. Galene spoke. "We are Du Heleanova fa du Riella. If you wish to test us," Galene's smile became a bit bitter, "then by all means, do." As one, they flicked their wrists, and the five elemental spheres spun towards each other, melding into a brief torrent of Earth, Air, Fire, Water, and Ether, glowing brightly and exploding in a bright flash of light, leaving behind five charms in its wake, each of the element's symbols. The Heleanova took them, wearing them on a chain that appeared on their wrist.

Melete stepped forward. "Why?" she asked Galene softly. "Why did you leave?"

Galene pulled her into a rough embrace. "I'm sorry," she whispered. Dhara looked away, feeling like an intruder. There was nothing he could do to block out the words, though. "Grandfather, he told us to find our weapons and complete our task, to finish our duty. I had to go. I'm sorry, I'm so sorry," she kept saying, until they both could let each other go.

"Now," Galene straightened, "what makes you think it is poison?"

Draven cleared his throat. "We tested your grandfather's blood for poison," he said, "And it came back positive."

Galene waited. "For?" she finally asked.

"Hemlock." Draven hesitated. "It was a very unusual form of Hemlock. Almost as though he swallowed two dozen leaves ten months ago. It didn't make any sense."

Galene frowned. "He could've been poisoned ten months ago – his inheritance would've held it off – but why would he swallow them in the first place?"

Dhara decided to speak up. "I should be sure when I see the report, but it isn't Hemlock." He waited a moment for it to sink in. "At least, not purely hemlock. I haven't read the recipe for the poison, but I know it contains Aconite for subtlety, and Belladonna to soothe. Its symptoms are similar to hemlock, but not quite the same, like Mr. Alwood's were."

Galene turned back to Draven. "Could we see the report?" She asked.

Draven nodded. "Elethia?" he said, nodding to the person in question.

She handed over the report to Dhara, who nodded his thanks and turned to the page that covered cause of death.

"We usually don't have such detailed results in the general report, but this was an unusual case," said Draven, nodding towards Dhara.

Dhara didn't pay any attention to him. "Galene," he called, frowning. He thrust the file at her, frowning at the image of the blood work in the report. "Do you see that?"

Galene glanced at the report and paled. "Impossible," she whispered, fingers lightly touching the sheet, eyes alight with incredulity. "Absolutely impossible."

"What is?" demanded Elethia, finally, exasperated with their declarations.

Galene ceremoniously ignored her. "Do you have enough blood left for one more test?"

Draven hid a smile at the silent rebuke directed at Elethia. "Two more. Would you like to come there, or do you have equipment here?"

Galene smiled dryly. "Here is best. We have grounding here, the connection needed for our power to be at the highest potential."

"I thought so," he said, bringing out a vial from his pocket. At Galene's questioning look, he said, "We thought that she," he nodded towards Elethia, "could get a better connection here on scene."

Galene nodded, taking the vial. She placed it at the center of the room, where it floated in mid air, held up by Aura's gentle but firm winds. At Galene's nod, Caelus shifted the blood in the phial, separating the alien substances from it. Dhara took these substances into another vial, and Caelus calmed the lifeblood of their mentor. Dhara now analyzed the substances in the new flask, separating the poisons from the other substances.

Yes, poisons. The Lavena, for that was what the potion was called, consisted of several of the most poisonous substances in the world, which Dhara now separated. Once done, he passed control to Galene, who identified the function of each poison, understanding the potion the way only a master could. She had an eye for things that everybody ignored. She separated things that Dhara missed – here a grain's worth of Ricin, there a sliver of mandrake's root – small details that could have meant life rather than death for the old Helianov.

Finally, she gave passed the vial to Despione,

and she, calmly taking proportional amounts of the poison, remade it, finding out how it came to their mentor, essentially solving the last part of the mystery, putting together the puzzle for which the others had given the pieces. Aura gently helped her, drifting around her and making the pieces fall into place.

And soon, it was over.

CHAPTER 17

"Interesting," mused Caelus, looking at the small phial with an intensity that was new to anybody who knew him.

Of course, Dhara knew what he meant. It was very interesting. They detected a pattern so deep and intricate that it seemed almost impregnable. And yet, it had an inkling of familiarity, a brush of trust, a small nudge that led to a massive leap in faith, and ultimately resulted in untimely disappointment.

In fact…

"Gale?" Aura's voice was shaky, like she recognized herself in the depths of that bottle of death. "Did you see-"

Galene nodded, looking equally shaky. "That pattern," she whispered, eyes wide. Then she spun around, storming to her little training target, pelting it with fireballs. "Why-did-I-miss-this!" she shouted, enunciating her each word with another bulls eye. Caelus went and stood next to her, grabbing her hands before she could chuck her next fireball.

"Talk to me," he said, looking into her eyes.

Galene extinguished her hands. "The pattern, it follows ours. A double bluff, like Air always loved. We look for everything except what we would do, thinking that our enemy would think we'd look for that. A trap so intricate, that she'd never expect us to get it." She flicked her wrist, clearing the arena.

"What are you talking about?" Dhara demanded, thoroughly confused. Yes, a double bluff, but by whom? Who knew them so well? Who was their enemy?

Galene smiled bitterly. "Cardea." She nodded to Aura. "Your predecessor."

Aura's voice turned as icy as the winter winds. "She is Helianov no longer."

Despione nodded in agreement. "She betrayed us. She doesn't deserve the title."

Galene shook her head. "There's nothing we can do about it. Only the Riella Ranve can reach to the Elements to remove her powers. I think they did, but she found a way to keep it even without the Elements' consent."

Dhara's back straightened. "That's what you were talking about the other day. The need to stop her."

Galene nodded. Caelus smiled warmly at her. "And stop her we will."

Dessie cleared her throat. "We need to get going then. The sooner we do this, the sooner we can start work."

Galene nodded again and turned to Melete. "I may need to go soon," she said, gripping her sister's shoulder. She hesitated, unsure. Finally, settled with two simple words. "Stay strong."

And they left.

"What's the plan?" questioned Dhara, excited beyond belief.

Galene grinned. "Yes, we're getting the Gis. Any ideas as to where it is?" Dhara gave her a look, and she laughed. "I know I gave the general description, but where exactly is it?"

Dhara rolled his eyes. "Let's find out, shall we?"

Aura raised her eyebrows. "Honestly, you two." She shook her head, and grinned. "Divæs[1]."

Dhara tensed, but his instincts told him he was going home. He straightened his back, and landed perfectly on his feet, standing next to his friends.

"Lead on, Dhar." Aura stepped aside, momentarily giving in to his leadership. His throat clogged up with gratitude. He knew how much it cost for her, for ve fa Vrar[2] to bow to va fa Finthé[3]. For the winds to submit to earth.

He nodded in acknowledgement, but when he stepped forward, he froze. "This is different," he

1 Hidden Earth
2 She of Air
3 He of Earth

said, and then sighed. "Anthres was suspicious of Cardea, but he couldn't very well be open about it. He couldn't say, all heirs of Air can't get through the protections. He decided to ban all those who'd already gotten their weapons, under the pretext that I must learn to become independent of the weapons."

Galene nodded. "Grandfather did say that he was the sharpest of the lot. It seems to be a trait in the Earth Heleanova."

Dhara grinned. "Thanks, Gale."

She became serious. "Dessie can come, right?"

Dhara nodded. "Yeah. Thank the Elements for small mercies."

Galene grinned and turned to Dessie. "Keep him in line," she said in a mock drill sergeant voice.

"Hey!"

"Yes ma'am!" Dessie saluted.

"*Hey*!" The others laughed at Dhara's mock indignation.

"But in all seriousness," said Caelus, "stay safe and don't do anything stupid."

Dessie raised her eyebrows. "So says Caelus Sprite. You invented stupid, bro." Now it was Caelus turn to sputter in mock indignation.

Finally, Dhara shook his head. "Coming, Dessie?"

She nodded, expression clearing. "Let's go."

And they walked into the dark expanses of the cavern together.

CHAPTER 18

"Any idea what to expect?" Dessie asked, looking around.

Dhara shook his head. "People have this opinion that the earth is the most predictable of the Elements. Actually, that would be the other three. You always know which direction they will flow. But with Earth, well, we don't flow. We are calm, and strike when it is least expected. And Ether," his voice trailed of.

"We are Ether." Despione finished, grinning. There was a brief pause. "But what could come for you to control? That seems to be the general pattern here."

"The Riella Ranve added their own touches to the defenses. That's the most important part. If we learn what it is they want to teach us, and learn to spread that message, then we're deemed worthy. The more important part, I feel, is spreading the awareness, rather than getting it. It's the easier part, since the only person you have to convince is yourself, and you know yourself better than anybody else."

Dessie smiled. "That was surprisingly profound for a boy," she teased.

Dhara shook his head, pretending to be disappointed. "You underestimate us boys too often, young Helianov." He said in mock reproach.

"Is that so, Dhara fa Finthé?" She asked, raising her eyebrow.

Dhara's reply was cut off by something he should've expected.

A brief tremor began, but it seemed to hide a lot of power behind it. "Dhar?" Dessie asked, stepping behind him so they could cover each other.

"Layers," he said, keeping his voice low. "He's woven a spell to slowly increase the intensity of the tremors, but suddenly, he'll increase the strength, so only I can control it. I think it was in case Cardea convinced any of the new heirs to do this. The spell tests the new Heir's trustworthiness, along with his strength."

Dessie tensed. "Then why," she whispered, her tone matching his for volume, "am *I* being scanned?"

Dhara felt his eyes widen, and he spun around, pulling Dessie down.

And not a moment too soon.

"Evarés[1]!" Dhara yelled. He threw up an earthen shield around Dessie, making sure she can break out

1 Ironically enough, it's earth's pet snake.

of it, but no one can break into it. Rather ingenious, even if he said it himself.

He raised his knife, focusing on channeling his power into his knife.

The Evarés got impatient, and attacked. Immediately, Dhara lashed out with his magic, making the floor of the cavern too smooth for the snake to glide on. Dhara walked around it, keeping his knife ready. Suddenly, Evarés hissed. That was his only warning.

Dhara leapt aside, barely dodging the Evarés venom. However, he couldn't completely avoid it. A bit of the poison singed his shoulder, and he hissed in pain. He threw up another shield, took a breath. He had to control the Evarés, but he didn't know how. And judging by his shoulder, it wasn't easy.

He glanced at the weapon in his hands, and wondered. *They all come from the earth*, he thought, *so can they be changed to other forms?*

He concentrated on it, giving himself another weapon, one which he was more used to, which was made for him.

He made the Gis.

The shields shattered, and the Evarés silently slithered up to him, submitting to him. He glanced up at Dessie, confused.

He glanced to the copy of the Gis in his hands, and gasped. "Impossible," he whispered, tracing his hands along the Gis.

For that is what it was. The true Gis.

"Not impossible," smiled Earth. "Never impossible."

Fire glided down, laying a hand on his shoulder. "You needed this, and you made it. You displayed confidence, and a cool head even when you couldn't be sure of the next step."

"You became worthy of it when you refused to rely on it." Water smiled.

"It is the most important lesson you can learn," said Air.

Ether turned to Dessie. "And you stayed with them throughout. You learnt the importance of loyalty. And now, you have earned the final weapon."

The Riella Ranve disappeared in a flash of light, leaving behind three things: A gem of silver topaz, a stone of purple zircon, and the Caelum.

Chapter 19

"What's the plan?" asked Aura, flopping down on a cushion in the tent.

Dhara straightened. "Well, I thought we-"

"Not here!" hissed Galene, furious. "She was the Heir of Air. Obviously, she still has some power over it! Every small whisper we breath, flies back to her in an instant! Every word we utter, every sentence we mutter, everything goes back to her! Making plans in the open air is a *bad* idea!"

Caelus nodded. "She's right. What about the Enva?"

Galene shook her head. "It's still through air. A lot faster, quieter, and more convenient, but through air nonetheless."

Suddenly, the air around them stilled. Galene tensed, feeing the air around them for magic, and relaxed. "Sorry, 'Ra," she said, shaking her head. "But unless you can keep a bundle of air together for every moment we spend planning, and don't release it once we're done, there's no point."

"And visual?" questioned Dessie, frowning.

"No good," Aura offered. "I tried it, and, fortunately or unfortunately, it worked."

Dhara frowned. "But won't the wind currents touch a lot of things? Won't that bring in an overload of information?"

Aura shook her head. "Think of the layers of air as filters. We tell the layer next to us what we need, and that layer tells the next, and so on, until the last layer finds all the necessary information. The previous layers sort of compare it with the conditions for the information, and reject a few. Finally, you have only three or four left, and the winds get to work. It can't exactly be seen, but its path can be traced. It 'draws' the image onto the ground. One color only, unless you happened to spill ink in, in which case it'll become abstract art."

Galene frowned. "'Ra," she began, eyes wide, "can *you* get information that way?"

Aura shrugged. "Sporadically. I've tried thrice, it's worked once."

Galene nodded absently. A communication system, perhaps…

She shook her head. These thoughts were useless now.

"But we can't barge in without a plan because we're scared she'd know it! That's utter madness!" cried Aura, staring at Galene.

Galene nodded. "But she can't control the other Elements, now, can she?"

Aura frowned. "But we can't control the other Elements either!"

Galene glanced at Caelus. He grinned. "Looks like clumsy is the new fancy!"

Galene shook her head, smiling. "Idiot," she said fondly. "If Dessie gives the girls permission, and Cal gives Dhar permission, we can get some sort of coordination going. I-"

Despione interrupted. "How do you know that my realm is out of hers?" She demanded.

Galene shrugged. "I did some research. I'll take you to a star if it'll compensate," she said. "In fact, it'll be neutral ground. After all, a star is a big ball of burning gases in the middle of Ether's realm."

Dessie's shoulders slumped. "Why," she said wryly, "am I not surprised?" Her eyes went skyward.

Galene laughed. "Star it is, then. I'll make the fire repel her, and you take care of the ether."

Dessie nodded. Galene turned to Dhara and Caelus. "Meet you in the ocean. See you in two!"

Galene nodded to Dessie, and they disappeared.

Three seconds later, they opened their eyes. "Wow." Galene stared around, startled.

"This," started Aura.

"Is," continued Dessie.

"Epic!" they finished together.

Galene glanced at them, disgruntled. "What is with you two and twin speak?"

They laughed. "I have a question," said Dessie.

"Shoot," said Galene, nodding.

"Why do we need to split the groups if we're going to give the groups permission anyway?"

"If all the five Heleanova gathered at one place, then any of the previous Heleanova can come to that place."

Dessie raised an eyebrow. "So she could've been to any of the places we've been to?"

Galene nodded. "I doubt it, though," she reassured the two. "With the five of us there, we could have sensed her."

Aura interrupted them before they could go any further. "So, the plan?"

Galene nodded. "Here's what we're going to do..."

And so they planned.

Chapter 20

Nasr cowered against the wall, terrified of the woman in front of him.

"How did they know?" demanded the woman, her hands resting delicately on the scry-bowl in front of her. "Even Andy didn't know!"

Nasr stepped forward. "Andy, Mistress?"

"Andres, you fool, Andres Alwood! The Helianov Andres Alwood!" She stared into the bowl, forcing the wind to dance in the water, making it paint its images in the liquid. It had learnt not to resist. "How did she know?"

She shook her head, and glared at the cowardly little vulture. "Glean what information you can from them," she ordered him. "Get whatever you can." Her hand shot out, catching the bird before he could leave. She stared into his eyes with her own silver ones. They pierced the vulture's own sharply. "Do not disappoint me, Nasr."

"Of course, mistress," said the little creature, the picture of subservience.

She nodded, and raised her arm. "Go."

He left.

The pale woman rose. "I will get you yet, Heleanova!" she swore, her pale eyes flashing with a dangerous promise, her light hair flying in the wind. She raised her arms, her flowing dress falling with grace. "I will get you yet!" She sent out a shot of lightning, as a warning, telling them that they will soon be hers. Soon.

And Galene awoke with a gasp.

"You're sure that's what you saw?"

"Yes, Dhara," Galene snapped, glaring at the said Helianov. "And if you ask me again, you'll see why I'm the Helianov of Fire!"

Dhara raised his hands up in defense. "Just making sure, Gale." He shook his head. "This is bad," he began.

"Now, who could have thought?" snapped Galene sarcastically.

"But what did she mean?" Dhara finished, ignoring her outburst.

Galene shrugged, and said, "Let's just continue, shall we?"

Caelus nodded. He closed his eyes, and summoned a small swirl of water, just tall enough to consume him.

And he disappeared.

Galene closed her eyes, and focused on the core of her powers. It was, when calm, a small, blue-white sphere of fire, but when she used her Elemental inheritance, as she was going to now, the core grew into a large, pure white, burning ball of fire, destroying any other tendrils of power that wandered towards her, except, it seemed, the Heleanovan powers.

When she saw her core now, however, she stopped short in surprise. It was, not just a ball of fire, but a dance between fire and water, now flying together, now spinning apart, but forever connected by at least the smallest of bonds, the lightest of threads, the lowest of flames, the calmest of waters – they were joined. *Caelus,* she realized.

She pulled onto some fire, and concentrated on her grandfather's study, and released the fire. When she opened her eyes, she stood there. She straightened, brushing a few stray ashes from her shoulders.

And was promptly knocked down by a black ball known as Melete.

"You made it!" she cried, her eyes an odd mix of happiness, sadness, relief, and a hint of anger. "Did you get her?" They both knew whom she meant.

Galene shook her head. "Nope." Then- "Made it to what?"

Melete lowered her head. "Grandfather's funeral."

Galene turned away, refusing to let her tears flow. She had to stay strong for Melete.

Caelus stepped forward, holding Galene's shoulder. "Would you mind greatly if the rest of us," he nodded to the Heleanova, "came as well? He was our teacher, and a better one we couldn't have wished for."

Melete's eyes widened. "Oh, would you?"

"Of course," said Aura, her clothes changing to a somber, dark grey dress that looked like the darkest storm in the night, with the Astrapí strapped to her back.

Galene looked down, changing her clothes to a black dress, with Shadowfire at the bottom. It danced a dark dance, weaving a promise for justice. The Pyrós sat at her waist, announcing to whoever knew, that this was Galene fa Pyra, Helianov of Fire.

The other Heleanova changed their clothes to mourning as well, and they stepped out in a V formation, with Galene and Melete at the tip, Caelus and Dhara behind them, and Despione and Aura behind them. They walked to the old Helianov's funeral.

The guests parted to leave them a path for the Heleanova. Galene knelt next to her grandfather, and the other Helianov soon followed suit. Melete stepped back, head bowed, and tears streaming freely down her face.

Galene spoke, hissing out a promise in Pyropathos that only she understood.

"§*You will be avenged, Grandfather. This I swear.*§"

She rose in unison with the others, and turned to face the crowd. She glanced at Melete for approval, and waited. Finally, agonizingly slowly, she nodded.

"People of the Elements!" Galene called, getting the few whisperers to quiet down. "It is our tradition, that when a Helianov dies, he is to be sent to the other world with his Element. I ask you all, may we do this?" The crowd muttered their assent. "I thank you."

Galene turned back, and drew the Pyrós.

"§*Be Free,*§" she whispered, her words flying over the voices of the wind. She called the fire from the Pyrós to touch their old master one last time. And then-

"Be free," whispered the other Heleanova, watching the ashes scatter in the wind, knowing that that's what was needed.

"Be free," echoed the people, sealing the promise.

And the Heleanova turned and left.

CHAPTER 21

In the next few days, the Heleanova set up their center in their old training room, creating a map of the known worlds, the ones they had visited, the ones others had. They knew that before they could attack, they had to have a good defense. The house itself was well defended, of course, but the rest of the world ought not be caught in the war.

War, thought Galene. *I never thought that I would be involved in one so soon after our acceptance. I never thought about it at all.*

"It's funny how things turn out, isn't it?"

Galene nodded without turning. "Cal."

Caelus came and sat down, reaching over and providing the silent comfort that she had come to depend on. *Stay strong.* He told her through the bond.

What if I can't? Asked Galene, sighing. She'd never felt so weak, so scared.

Caelus held her hands, staring into her eyes with his own, their song singing, ever so subtly, a song of hope, and trust, and strength, and she drew from it her own. She trusted him, and he trusted her. They relied on each other, and on everybody else.

"There you are!"

The two Heleanova jumped. "Don't do that, Mel!" said Galene, hand over her racing heart.

Melete grinned teasingly. "Did I scare you?"

Galene straightened. "No," she said, her voice mock arrogant. "Never!"

Melete giggled, and shook her head. "'Ra's calling you. She says it's important."

Galene stood up, pulling Caelus up as well. "I'd best go see what she wants, then."

Melete nodded. "You know where she is, obviously."

Galene grinned, and ran to the study, throwing open the door. "You called, 'Ra?"

"Wards, Galene." With those two words, Galene's entire demeanor changed. She raised her hands, whispering a spell to protect them, raising shields around the house to help them:

Eviar Vriar, Avas Harsiv, Bruwe Finthé,

Josrov Pyra, Heva Ethella,

Nar du Rasuv, Nar du Maeru,

Nar Fe Ka Twa du Travst fa Kastag.[1]

The protections built up; with each Element covering for the other, layering over one another and ensuring that there were no holes in the defense. The Elements were, then, truly one.

"Did you find anything?" Asked Galene, stepping forward.

Aura nodded. "It's about our charms."

"What about them?"

Aura grinned. "Two words, Gale. Secret chambers."

Galene grinned back. "Awesome!"

"And get this," interjected Dhara, his eyes dancing with excitement. "Its warded against everybody except the current Helianov of the Element, and the Element himself, or herself."

Galene raised her eyebrows. "They're for each individual Helianov?" She asked, surprised. Dhara nodded. "Interesting," she murmured. It was a mixed blessing, in that it would grant them some

1 A short spell that roughly translates to: Gentle Breeze, Rough Sea, Calm Earth, Fierce Fire, Quiet Ether Protect the knowledge, Protect the People, Protect us all from the wrath of Evil. Not very spell like, but then again, it's only a rough translation.

privacy, but it might drive a wedge between them. With this group, however, that might be a tad difficult. Galene shook her head, and then grinned. "Wanna explore?"

Aura pointed at the floor, where their elements once spun together. "Check it out."

Galene knelt on the ground, and saw five symbols on the ground – the Heleanovan symbols, to be precise. She traced her own, following the crimson letter with her eyes. Raising her hand, she brushed the rune with her fingers, lightly touching the symbol. It glowed with power, steadily pulsing brighter and brighter, until it grew too bright for the others to see. She felt them turn away, but she looked on. It was fire. It wasn't too bright for her.

And slowly, the blaze died down, leaving behind only the slightest gleam, just enough to know that something had happened. She looked up, eyes searching for what, she didn't know, until she saw it.

There, wreathed in flames, was an entrance into another home.

Another home, she thought, her face smiling ever so slightly. *I only wish I won't be quite so alone.*

"I'll be back soon," she said as she walked towards the door.

And the flames flew behind her, clasping her in a warm, fiery embrace that made her feel safe, calm, and content. She stepped forward, letting the flames shroud her in their soothing clasp.

She turned around the earthen chamber. There was a small fireplace, burning brightly, casting a warm glow on the room. The room was simply furnished, with a couch in front of the fireplace, a desk, and two chairs. On the walls, there were two paintings, one of her own, and the other –

"Pyra," she breathed, staring at the portrait. If it was accurate, then Pyra looked a lot like her heirs. Or rather, her heirs looked a lot like her.

"Galene," came a whisper, echoing around the room.

Galene spun around, drawing the Pyrós, heart thudding loudly in her chest. *I thought only Pyra and her heirs could come here,* she thought, eyes scanning the room. Suddenly, there was a burst of fire in the middle of the room, too bright for her to see. *And if it's too bright for me,* she thought wryly.

"My Heir."

Those two words were enough to send her to her knees, submitting to her Lady. The being in front of her exuded power beyond imagination. Galene kept her eyes down, waiting for acknowledgement from her.

From Fire.

"My heir," she said again, her voice like the whispering furnaces in the dead of the night, not rough, but not smooth, not harsh, but not soothing, an eerie mix of beauty incomprehendable. She brushed Galene's shoulder, pausing momentarily over the tunic. Fire licked Galene's form, but still she didn't move.

"Rise," said Pyra finally, stepping back. "Look up, child," she chided softly. "You mustn't go against your nature, and I suppose you are not naturally submissive."

Galene looked up, grinning. "That's true, my Lady."

Pyra grinned back. "That's all me, I'm afraid." She sat on one of the two chairs in front of the fireplace, gesturing for Galene to sit in the other. "I suppose you are wondering why I came here."

"It crossed my mind, my Lady, yes," said Galene, trying to stay at least a little respectful.

Pyra smiled like she knew exactly what she had been thinking. Galene tensed, heat rushing into her cheeks. *If she does,* she thought.

"This fight," began Pyra, "is more vital than you may now realize. It will be…" she hesitated, then sighed. "I cannot say. You need to emerge victorious, but we cannot interfere."

Galene stared. How could this small matter – well, small to them, anyway – be so important that Pyra came and visited her heir, and even considered interfering?

"But we can help," Pyra interrupted her speculations again. She raised her arms, and the flames that had been lingering on her momentarily brightened, as though remembering an old tune, a forgotten dance.

And the flames vanished, leaving behind on her form a set of Armor.

It fit her perfectly, with a fiery red comb on the golden helmet, and golden armor plates. Right in the middle of the breastplate was a lone flame, the symbol of Pyra – the small fire of hope that burns when all is hopeless.

"Touch that," said Pyra, "and the suit shrinks into a pendant that carries my insignia. That, and the Pyros, you can never lose."

"Thank you, my Lady," said Galene, overwhelmed.

"Burn bright, my heir. Burn always, and even your enemies shall turn away in awe of your power."

So saying, she left in a flash of flame, leaving behind a million questions at the tip of Galene's tongue.

Chapter 22

Galene shrunk the armor, and looked around. On the desk, there was a lone book, in a faded red leather cover, looking like a book much loved, much read. Galene picked it up, reading the name emblazoned on the leather in beautiful golden letters. It was not in English. It wasn't even in Lenaula.

It was in Pyrapath.

§*The True Fire.*§ Pyra's secrets, her knowledge, and perhaps a lot more, in this one book, for Galene to know, and, more importantly, understand. She opened the book, and read.

"I found something," she told the others later.

"Really?" asked Aura wryly. "I would have never guessed."

"A book," she said, ignoring Aura's interruption. "called 'The True Fire', written in Pyrapath. There was a passage in it that caught my attention."

She handed over a sheet to Dhara, who scanned it before his eyes shot up. "Gale, this is *huge*."

"Ya think?" she asked sarcastically. "Read it out."

Dhara cleared his throat. "Pyra's heirs have always had a fiery temper, true to their Lady's nature. This fire, eventually, lead to their fall.

"But one Helianov, whose real name has been long forgotten, once tamed this storm. Firetamer, he was called, for he, instead of calming the fire within, he used it, *tamed* it, and with his anger, his ardor, his True Fire, he destroyed his enemies."

There was a pause, in which everyone turned to Galene. "How did he do it?" Asked Caelus, finally.

"I don't know. But I must learn." Galene extended her hand, letting fire envelop the paper and drift along her hand. "This fire," she said, staring at the flames that danced across her palm, "is not that of hate, or anger. It's of love, but if I think of Grandfather, or Cardea," The flames turned black, and then became a small, lone tongue of the fiery emotions in her heart. "It becomes Blackfire. This fire, it's the fire of hate, of deep, irrepressible anger." She clenched her fist, extinguishing the Blackfire. "I may not be able to control it, which is why I don't use it."

"What about that fire that you used before the funeral?" asked Dessie.

"That was Shadowfire, the fire of promise. The other dark colored fire is Darkfire, the fire of pain, of hurt. When a fire Helianov is hurt, this fire is the result. It rests in the heart of the Helianov, with the other fires, dark and light, waiting to be released."

"How?" asked Dessie, her eyes shining, as though all the galaxies in the world were shining through them.

"Soulfire," whispered Galene. "I don't know my heart, so I dare not use it."

Caelus held her hand, looking into her eyes with his own. "But we do," he whispered, eyes swirling with both his magic and hers. "Try," he said, releasing her hand.

Galene took a deep breath, and cupped her hands. She summoned a fist full of fire, focussing on her heart. She remembered her anger at Cardea, her pain at the death, her promise to bring justice, her sorrow at the loss, her happiness at her friends, her love towards her sister.

And she thought of Caelus, the way his eyes sang with her power, his power, her fire, now his fire, his storm, now her storm, and she finally accepted the part of him that was now her. She accepted it.

That she loved him.

And her fire glowed black with her pain, anger, and promise. It was a deep red with her sorrow, and a bright gold at her happiness. It was a beautiful with her love towards her sister. And blue and green with her love towards Caelus.

The others stared at it, except one.

Caelus looked at her, and she held her breath, dare not hoping that he did too, that he cared for her the same way that she did him.

He extended his arm, bringing from his heart his song, his music, his melody, the part of her that was him – the part of him that was her.

Or were they both, the same? For in the midst of all the fire, there was a soft song, a song of his love for her, a song of her love for him.

His heart, his song, it was his sorrow at her pain, his fear for her refusal, his happiness at her light, his love for her fire. And in his heart was her name. Not Galene Alwood, not Galene fa Pyra, just Galene. He loved her for her, not for who she pretended to be. He knew her strength, her weakness, her sorrow, her faith.

And she loved him for it.

Her eyes found his, and with that song, that dance, they accepted each other. They accepted the others pain, sorrow, promise, hope, and most importantly, love.

And now, they were one.

And that was what mattered.

Galene poked her head into the training room. "Hey, Cal," she said, searching for him. He emerged from the fire part of the room, absently extinguishing some other fires. "Yeah?" he asked.

"I'm going to go see if there are any breakthroughs in the case." She said, her eyes smoldering with her fury. "Wanna come?"

To make sure I don't lose control.

But that went unsaid.

Caelus nodded. "Get the rest of the fire, will you?" He said casually, like he was asking her to get the keys. Galene swept her arm, collecting the fire, and pulled it to her hand. Closing her fist, she extinguished it. "Ready?"

He nodded, and they left.

But hardly a few minutes had passed when they were stopped.

"Galene Alwood, Caelus Sprite. We finally meet."

Galene spun around, raising a shield of fire and water as she did. She spoke, her voice filled with intense fury. "Cardea."

CHAPTER 23

Cardea laughed mockingly. "Now, now, is that any way to speak to a lady? What ever would your grandfather say, young Helianov?"

"He'd be glad I'm not falling for your foolish attempts at trickery," she retorted, forcing herself to remain calm.

"What do you want, Cardea?" demanded Caelus, his voice guarded.

Cardea laughed again, her voice filling the air. "To talk, of course," she said, spreading her arms. Three chairs appeared from thin air, upon one of which she sat, her light hair falling delicately from her shoulders, her hands resting on her lap. For all appearances, she was a gentle lady, except for her eyes.

The eyes of a predator.

Galene swept her hands, summoning two chairs, one of fire, and one of ice. "I'm sure you understand our reluctance to trust, Cardea fa du Gvan."

Cardea of the fallen. For those who lost, those who betrayed.

Her eyes flashed with anger. "Not yet, Galene Alwood. It will be you, not I. This I promise."

The words chilled her heart, but she dispelled the fear. Fear was not an option. Not now. "Is that so," she questioned mockingly, placing her hands gently on the armrests of her chair.

"One against five?" questioned Caelus lightly, mockingly. "Doesn't seem too fair, does it?"

Cardea smiled. "Yes," she whispered softly. "To you."

Galene tilted her head, letting a soft, feral smile play on her lips. "Is that so, Cardea?" She leaned back, for all appearances, completely at ease. "Well, you'd best buckle up," she began.

"-'Cause you're in for a huge surprise." Finished Caelus. "Believe me," he continued, "You don't know what you're up against."

Cardea laughed. "You honestly believe you can stand up against me? Five little children," she sneered, "with the barest grasp on their powers, up against the Air's strongest beasts?"

The two Heleanova rose, standing shoulder to shoulder, fire and ice dancing together in complete harmony, presenting a dauntless image for any who stands against them. "Well," said Galene, glancing at Caelus, trying to tell him to be ready. "The odds of our winning-"

"-Is much better then yours."

Cardea rose, smiling. "We shall see." From behind rose two dark birds. "They used to say," she continued, "that Huginn and Muninn are ravens." The birds shrieked in anger. "That would be incorrect. They are the Evaar[1]. My Evaar."

The birds were completely black, except for their startlingly electric blue eyes, and a silver symbol on their chest. On one was the Lenaulan letter H, and on the other was the Lenaulan letter M:

"I'll just leave you to play, then, shall I?" Cardea smiled, and disappeared in a gust of wind.

Caelus glanced at Galene. "You take Huginn, I'll take Muninn?"

Galene shook her head. "No," she said. "We're stronger together too." Hopefully stronger than them.

Hopefully.

1 Legendary birds born from the blood of Air spilt during the First War. They are unbeatable together, but separate, they are vulnerable.

Caelus drew the Kÿma, dropping into a fighting stance. Galene drew the Pyrós, and summoned a ball of water. She threw it behind her, towards the house. Caelus sent a questioning glance towards her.

"Aura," she said shortly. "No sudden movements," she ordered him. "Don't attack."

"Excuse me?"

Galene rolled her eyes. Boys. "Maybe Aura can help us out, in that they were born from Air, and she is the Heir of Air. No, not a word."

The two birds circled them, ready to attack. They were waiting for the first move, the first attack.

What's wrong? demanded Aura.

Huginn and Muninn. Replied Galene. *I thought that maybe you, being the Heir of Air, could stop them.*

No, she said. *They were born from destruction, and hence can only live thus. We're almost there.*

"Ready?" said Galene, getting into their defensive position, just as Aura, Dhara and Dessie came in. The others gave their affirmations. "Now."

Galene spun around, swinging the Pyrós. A jet of white-hot flames shot out from the blade. A ring of fire rushed towards the birds, and they shot up. Raising her arms, she raised the ring up, trying to get the birds. The birds dodged, shooting down towards the Heleanova. Aura shot an arrow towards Huginn, and the two birds moved away, their movements synchronized as though they were not two immortals, but one.

Which they sort of were.

Dhara, info! demanded Galene.

Ok, he thought, heart racing. *Born from the blood of Air when Fire cut him. They are practically unbeatable together-*

But they have been, right? asked Aura, her voice, for lack of a better word, hopeful.

Yes. But…

Spit it out. snapped Galene, shooting out a jet of fire and water from her hand, sending it spiraling towards Muninn.

It was the Elements united.

Well, we have all the Heleanova here, and we are together-

No. Dhara interrupted, simultaneously trying to stab Huginn in the wing. *The Elements, as in,* ***the Elements***.

"Hellfire!" cursed Galene, summoning a ball of Shadowfire, sending it spiraling towards both the birds.

"That would be Shadowfire," said Caelus cheekily, sending a ball of sea green waters after the fireballs.

"Hilarious."

"I know, right?"

Dessie interrupted Galene's retort. "You guys can flirt later. There's a fight going on, in case you forgot."

"We're not flirting!" snapped the two said teens.

How did they do it? demanded Galene, returning to the original subject.

Nerra[1].

"Maybe they'll help," said Aura, her voice not quite so hopeful now.

Galene shook her head. "We can't expect interference. We're on our own."

Now that's a depressing thought.

Suddenly, there was loud shriek, and the birds swooped down on Aura. Huginn swiped with his – her? – claw, and Aura fell. "Aura!" cried Galene, grabbing her before she could hit the ground. She was out cold. Galene looked up, furious. She spun the Pyrós in one hand, and ran towards the birds. "§*Darkfire!*§" she commanded in Pyropathos. "§*Blackfire! Shadowfire! Heartfire*[2]*! Stormfire*[3]*!*§" She continued. She took a deep breath, and uttered the last command. "§*Soulfire!*§" The five fires burnt together, forming a deadly dance. Black flames danced across her palm, mixing with the deep red of Heartfire and the beautiful emerald of Stormfire.

---

1 Pure forms. The elements in their rawest, most dangerous beauty

2 Fire of love, friendship, family

3 Water's fire

The fire coated her body, dancing along the blade of the Pyrós - no, it became the blade. She ran towards the birds, ducking as Muninn swung his claw at her. She swiped the Pyrós up, cutting his hand as she passed. She spun to avoid Huginn's beak, and, sweeping her arm, she sent a jet of flames towards the birds. Not faltering, she rolled and stabbed at Huginn's wing, simultaneously shooting a jet of fire at Muninn. A few moments later, she realized Caelus was fighting by her side, shooting jets of water and sweeping the Kÿma as though he'd done it all his life. Together, they fought the Evaar, stronger together as well.

A disk whizzed past them, covered in the dark power of Ether. Dessie spun another disk out towards Huginn, and the bird dodged, flying towards her. Muninn followed closely behind, closing in on Dessie. She caught her first disk when it flew back to her, and she spun it to veer Muninn off course. Huginn continued flight, and Dessie rolled as he flew over her. She caught both the disks, and spun around, catching Huginn twice on the chest. She leapt back, narrowly missing the furious beast's beak. Galene turned to Muninn, spinning her dagger in her hand. She ran towards the bird, shooting a stream of Soulfire at him. Ducking, she thrust the Pyrós up into the bird's chest, right where his heart must be. Immediately, she was pushed back, thrust away from beast by a gust of wind. Galene braced herself, and ran towards the creature. Leaping up, she tried to reach it's back.

She missed.

"Oh, hellfire!" she cursed.

"Gale!" yelled Caelus.

"Wait!" she called, concentrating on Muninn.

She hung on to his foot, pulling till she got a better hold. Slowly, laboriously, she climbed up, taking care to not get kicked off. The fall promised to be painful.

Finally, she reached the creature's back. Taking a deep breath, she raised the Pyrós, which she had miraculously kept a grip on, and brought it down in a flash of black flames. Thrusting her power out, she sent flames raging into the bird, burning out every bit of Cardea's influence. Finally, she thrust her Soulfire into the bird, knowing it was as close to Nerra as she could get. It was truly her. Hesitating, she closed her eyes, and sent in streams of water. The part of her that was him.

Getting a bit old, hmm? True nonetheless.

And opening her eyes – when did she close them? – she gazed at Muninn. What was left of him, anyway.

"Huginn?" she demanded once she caught her breath. Wordlessly, Caelus pointed at another pile of ashes. Galene grinned. "Yeah, Dess!" she cheered.

Dessie shook her head. "It wasn't me. It was you."

CHAPTER 24

"Me?" repeated Galene. "What- how-" she stammered. *Impossible. I was taking care of Muninn.* "That's a *really* bad joke."

"It's not a joke," said Dhara. "You did it. You achieved Nerra."

Galene's eyes widened. "But I'm not an Element! I don't have Nerra!" she snapped, confused.

"You do," said Dhara, shaking his head. "Or at least something similar to it."

"How?" She asked. Could it have something to do with what Pyra told me? The greater threat? Or is it something else entirely?

She shook her head. "Let's just head home."

"Do you want to check the progress they've made with the case?" asked Caelus.

Galene shook her head. "We'll take care of that later."

Caelus nodded, and they headed home.

"Oh God, Gale!" said Melete, horrified. "What happened?"

"Attack." She replied, a bit tired. "Nothing much, but I need to do some research."

"Nothing much!" snapped Melete, glaring. "You're bruised, the other's are cut, and Aura's knocked out! What's 'much', then?"

Galene blinked, startled. "Your sister, Gale," said Caelus finally. "She's truly your sister."

"Huginn and Muninn." said Galene.

Melete's eyes widened. "You're trying to tell me that two ravens did this to you?"

Galene shook her head. "Myths. Huginn and Muninn are most definitely not ravens. Or any other small birds. They're huge."

"Were." said Dessie. "Any ideas how you did it?"

Galene shook her head. "I'm going to see if there's anything about it in 'The True Fire'. Take care of Aura, will you? My fire can't heal just yet." She could feel it simmering beneath her surface, ready to lash out.

"You OK?" asked Melete, concern lacing her voice.

Galene nodded. "I'm good. How're you holding up?"

Melete smiled softly. "Better now you're here," she murmured, hugging her sister tightly.

Galene's throat tightened. *Me too, Mel,* she thought. *I'm glad you're here for me.* She took a deep breath, and closed her eyes. *I promise I'll always protect you. Always.*

"Now, how are you going to save the world?" asked Melete teasingly.

"No clue," joked Galene. "I'll go find out, shall I?" smiling, she turned to her chambers.

Inside, she glanced at the portrait of Pyra. *Help us,* she pleaded. *At least tell us what's going on. What's wrong with me? What was that? It wasn't Nerra, was it?* Galene closed her eyes, and bowed her head. "I know you can't interfere, but just give some sign, some signal, that nothing's wrong. No more than usual, at any rate," she added as an afterthought. Sighing, she turned. There was a door on the side, and she opened it. Immediately, she froze. The amount of protections she felt there, it was amazing. She slowly stepped through, unsure.

The room was dark, with a lone lantern burning near the door. She summoned a ball of bright fire, scanning the room. Glancing to the side, she saw another lantern. She shot a bit of flame to it, lighting it. The entire room lit up, with five lanterns to the right and five to the left. On the opposite wall, there were six practice dummies, each wielding a different weapon. At the center, there was a ring with ten targets on the edge. Upon closer inspection, the targets would reconstruct themselves automatically. The dummies would do that two, and one of them was even immune to fire. To it was stuck a note-

Fight without powers. If you should find yourself in a position where you can't use your powers, you should be prepared.

It wasn't signed, but the handwriting was familiar.

"Thanks, grandfather." She whispered.

Each of the other five dummies would be able to mimic the powers of one of the elements. That would be useful, but for now, she had to burn some fuel. She went to the center of the circle, and took a deep breath. She focused, and summoned a small ball of Blackfire. Rolling it in both palms, she rolled it in mid air, finally sending it rushing to the target in front of her.

Bulls eye.

A small note fluttered down, written on a piece of parchment in a bright red ink.

Be free.

She blinked at the old Heleanovan blessing. *It's true, I guess,* she thought. Be free.

Taking a deep breath, she summoned a larger ball of Blackfire, letting it engulf her. Spinning around, she sent balls of fire at all the targets. Sweeping her arms wide, she summoned three strips of fire.

Blackfire, Darkfire, and Shadowfire.

Concentrating, she brought the three flames together. They were all a part of her, but they warred. They competed for the ability to consume everything.

No, she thought, *you will consume* nothing, *least of all me.* She wove the fires together, forming a ring of the three fires – one pure black, the Shadowfire, one a touch gold, the Darkfire, and the other a touch red, the Blackfire. Reaching in, she pulled out a tongue of Heartfire and Stormfire, and wove it with the other stream. She closed her eyes, and carefully pulled out from her core shards of ice and streams of water, carefully weaving a sphere of power, entwining fire and water.

It was beautiful.

Bringing her arms together, she pulled the sphere smaller and smaller, until it fit in her palm. Raising her arm she threw it up, making it shoot jets of interwoven fires and icy waters all around, creating a cage of power that spread across the entire room. She tried to pull it all back into the sphere, but she lost control. The cage dissipated, and the sphere started falling down. Raising her hand, she quickly stopped the ball and instinctively forced it to disintegrate.

Taking a deep breath, she started again.

Controlling Soulfire.

CHAPTER 25

Galene lay on her bed, staring at the ceiling. It was going to happen soon, she knew. Were they ready? How crucial was this conflict? Why did the Elements even consider interfering?

Finally, she gave up on sleep, and climbed to the terrace. The mattress was still there, but this time, it was occupied.

"Hey, Cal," said Galene, sitting next to him.

"Galene," he nodded. There was a brief pause, and then Caelus sighed. "It's coming soon, right?"

Galene nodded. "Tomorrow, I think." She closed her eyes. "It seems too soon, but at the same time, too late."

Caelus nodded. "I know. What's the plan?"

Galene stared at the sky. "We wait, I guess."

Caelus sighed, and got up. "Try to sleep, Gale. You'll need it."

"I know, Cal." She lay down. "I know."

Caelus smiled, and went down to his room. After a few minutes, Galene followed his example and went to sleep, her dreams plagued by whispers and shades of zephyrs and flurries that seemed intent on blowing out any flames she summoned.

"So what's the plan?" asked Caelus, his eyes uncharacteristically serious.

"We know that she will have an assortment of creatures at least as vicious as the Evaar. Dhara and Aura, you two need to research on creatures. Find out what things we could be up against. Weaknesses, strengths, a bit of history. Anything you can find.

"Dessie, see if there's anything we can call to our aid. Any creature, person, magic – whatever can help us stop her. I'll come over and help both groups occasionally.

"Cal and I need to work on our fire and water powers respectively. It's an advantage – a small one, but an advantage nonetheless. Any questions?"

Aura nodded. "A few. Firstly, do I need to research?"

Galene rolled her eyes. "You are the Vrar Helianov. You know much more about the creatures of air than any of us. Considering who we're up against, it would be best to have you do this."

Aura nodded. "We also need a strategy. Who'll be doing what when the time comes."

Galene felt her anger rise. "Cardea is mine." She growled.

Dhara nodded. "It's the logical choice. No offence to you guys, but she's the most powerful of us."

Galene shook her head. "No, I have least control. Fire is difficult to constrain."

"And Air isn't?" demanded Aura, challenging.

Galene shook her head. "Watch."

Walking to her training area, she put up some of the wards from the room. "Pay attention to the red flame in particular, Caelus. If my guess is right, you have Heartfire."

Caelus nodded.

She called around her five globes of fire. Blackfire, Shadowfire, Darkfire, Heartfire, and Stormfire.

Her Soulfire.

She closed her eyes, and spun around, sending the five flames spiraling around, rolling towards the ward. Still spinning, she drew her hands closer, pulling the flames closer to her. She stopped, raising her arms. The five fires gathered above her head, forming a small ball of flames. Repeating what she'd done in practice, she tried to make a cage of fire, unbreakable by even the Heleanova. Then she tried to unravel it, slowly pulling the flames towards her.

The cage collapsed, and flames rushed towards her. Raising her hand, she stopped the flames, forcing them to dissipate.

Frustrated at the lack of progress, she summoned a huge ball of fire, and spinning towards the target, she threw it at the target with a yell.

Taking a deep breath, she calmed the flames around her. With a quick gesture, she deactivated the wards, and walked over to the others. "See what I mean?" she asked, gesturing. "I've practiced this trick several times, but I can't seem to dispel the cage without dispelling the fire. It always gets out of control at that stage."

Dhara shook his head. "My guess is that you did that all of last evening, after the battle, correct?" At her affirmative nod, he continued. "You were practicing with your powers when we arrived today. Judging by the state of the room, you'd been at it for two hours, taking a small break in the middle for breakfast. Now, you did a huge show for us again. After that, you summoned a humungous fireball and burnt that poor target to cinders. And you're not even breathing hard."

Galene turned red. "I have a good stamina?" she asked, uncertain.

Dessie laughed. "Face it, Gale – you're powerful. Why are you complaining?"

"I'm not," she protested. "I-"

"Then there's no problem, is it?" interrupted Dhara, grinning. "C'mon, Aura. We've got some research to do."

"When do we attack, mistress?" asked Nasr, standing beside Cardea.

She gazed at the Heleanovan sanctuary. She had seen the children enter the house – the protections of Air would be easy for her to pass, and that was their weakness. She, Cardea, was the most powerful Helianov alive. With his help, she managed to keep her own powers, and gain a bit of the other powers. Fire evaded her mastery, but no matter. She could overwhelm her easily. After all, she had done it to her predecessor.

But the timing had to be perfect. Nightfall would be perfect, she supposed, but it was part of Ether's domain. At least, that was what she gleaned from Agwé[1]. (The fool hadn't even realized than she had poisoned his drink, she thought absently.) But Nightfall would be the perfect time for many of her…soldiers.

"Nightfall," she said finally, turning back to her tent. She had three hours till attack.

"When can we expect them?" Dessie looked calm, as though they were not talking about a battle that could end the world as they knew it.

"Nightfall," replied Galene. How she knew, she couldn't tell, but she did. "What have you found?"

Dhara cleared his throat. "Her army will have rocs, cockatrices, Adze, Ala, and Futen."

1 Previous Ether Heleanov

"Who can we call upon for help?" asked Caelus, the fire in his eyes more visible than ever.

"Just three," replied Dessie. "The Phoenixes, the Xans, and the Evarés."

Galene closed her eyes. Typical. "Shall we call them, then?"

"There is something else," began Dessie, hesitant. "Arra."

Galene tilted her head, not recognizing the word. "Arra?"

"True familiars, I suppose. You will be able to call on yours."

"Just me?"

Dessie nodded. "An Arrum appears when she deems the Helianov worthy. The Nerra? It was a sign. Your power has increased exponentially. This is a sign of bonding. If you call, she will respond."

"Or he," reminded Dhara.

"Or he," agreed Dessie.

Galene nodded. "What will the Arrum be? Human, or Creature?"

Dessie shrugged. "Typically, for the Heirs of Fire, it's a Fire Phoenix. In a few rare cases, it's a Xan Pyra."

Galene nodded. "How do I call her? Or him," she added when Dhara opened his mouth.

"No clue," said Dessie.

Galene sighed and nodded. "I'll try, then." Closing her eyes, she searched her mind and core for signs of another bond. There was the one she had with the other Heleanova. Here the one with Caelus. There didn't seem to be any other.

Wait, what was that?

A small brush against another, unfamiliar mind. It was oddly familiar, though – a forgotten friend returning after a long voyage.

Such ludicrous fancies, came a soft voice through the bond.

Um, my Arrum? She asked, hesitant, unsure as to what to do.

I have a name, you know. Vesta. Use it.

Hi, Vesta. I'm Galene.

I know, she said, amused.

We, as in the Heleanova, and by extension the rest of the world, need some help. Could you come? We have not much other help, and we really need to-

Breathe, Galene! Honestly, do you ever breathe?

Well, considering I'm not using any breath while talking this way, I'd say-

Oh, ha ha. Cheeky.

You know it! So, can you come?

Yes. I'll bring some friends as well. The kids are right about you bonding, but what they don't realize is that they have as well.

So, more help?

Yes, child.

I'm not a child!

You are.

Not!

Are.

Not.

Are

Not- oh, hellfire! It doesn't matter. Just come here, will you?

Yes.

And in a bright flash of fire, there appeared a beautiful bird in front of her.

She had a rather exquisite, fiery shade of orange plumage, with golden wing tips and tail feathers. Her claws were tipped with sharp talons, and on her breast was Pyra's insignia. Her eyes were like Galene's own – a mix of topaz and sapphire – a sign of her wide realm of control. *You're a Janova*[1]*!* said Galene, astounded.

What did you think I was, a fish?

No, but she said-

There's always a first. And you are exceptionally powerful.

1 Birds that control more than one realm. They use these realms to transport themselves to places and to protect their chosen. All the Elements have Arra, all of whom are Janova

Thank you. And I'm not a child.

Vesta nipped Galene's ear lightly, letting out a soft, musical chirp, as though she was laughing. Spreading her wings, she flew up and settled on Galene's shoulder.

Galene looked up, grinning at the other Heleanova. "I must have forgotten to mention – you guys have bonded too."

"Yeah," Aura rolled her eyes. "Just a small detail. Nothing important." The five Arra laughed, their voices mixing together in a beautiful harmony of music.

"Everyone, this is Vesta, a Janova."

Vesta chirped a cheerful greeting.

Aura grinned. "This is Ninlil, Xan Anver[1]." The Xan twittered in greeting, lightning flashing in her wings as she flew around the room.

Caelus grinned. "Presenting Janova extraordinaire, Laran." Laran trilled in amusement, his eyes matching Caelus green and gold.

"Veles, Earth Phoenix." Veles spread his brown wings, joining Ninlil in flight.

Dessie stepped forward, her Arrum on her shoulder. "This is Asteria, Dark Phoenix."

"Veles stop flying here if you don't have room!" snapped Dhara, shaking his head. Veles trilled at him, and Dhara laughed.

---

1 Lightningbird

Veles has always been rather mischievous. I'm sure your enemies won't be expecting to be pranked into inaction by an ingenious Earth Phoenix.

I'll bet they won't, laughed Galene. *Can we call any other help?*

Vesta nodded. *The Earth Helianov can call Evarés. He will respond. You can also call the other Phoenixes and Xan.*

So I can call fire Phoenixes and Pyra Xans?

And the others call their respective Phoenixes and Xan. However, you can only call two of each. Or rather, only two will respond.

Galene nodded and turned to the others. "Let's call for reinforcements, then."

Closing her eyes, she reached out into the other worlds with her mind. *Phoenixes? Xan? We need help! We will soon be under attack! Can you help us?* She called, searching for the creatures.

We will come, came a deep voice.

There were four flashes of light, and two phoenixes and xans appeared.

We are the Yttre, said the Phoenixes.

We are the Invrar, chirped the Xan.

We will help you.

With that, the world exploded.

Chapter 26

"Hellfire!" cursed Galene, ducking as a roc swooped overhead. Veles attacked the said roc, flying around the remains of the room.

Actually, it was the remains of the house. Galene sent Melete and her aunt to Divæs, giving them protection while the battle raged on. The moment she'd turned back around, she spotted Cardea. She started towards her, but she was interrupted by the roc.

Trusting Veles to handle it, she continued forward. She glanced at the other Heleanova, and noticed something she hadn't before. Each of them had something with their Riella's insignia – ring, bracelet, earring, anklets, and her own pendant. The other Heleanova touched them presently, calling to their hands something extra to add to their arsenal.

Running forward with uncharacteristic aggression, Dhara speared one opponent and punched the other. Wait, punched? Oh, Bhag Nakh.

That would work for him, thought Galene. *Tigerfist, I guess, I should call him.*

Aura darted around, twirling gracefully with a Japanese war fan in each of her hands. There, she cut down an Ala, here fell a Futen. *That must hurt,* thought Galene. They were, after all, part of her domain.

Dessie – no, that was wrong. Despione twirled in her hands a Guan Dao, a pole weapon with a sword-like blade at the end. Finding no enemies around, she went to help Caelus.

And he was the picture of perfection, though she may be a little biased. He spun around a sling staff like he'd been wielding it his entire life, picking up random things from the ground, walls – wherever – and throwing them at the birds. On occasion, when the birds dropped rocks at them, he grabbed it and spun around, throwing it right back.

Galene's hand went to her throat, reaching her pendant. *No,* she thought, leaping forward to attack an Adze. *That would be too early.*

She glanced at Caelus again, slightly annoyed. *Why isn't he wearing armor? He isn't invincible!*

The other two girls were, sensibly, wearing their own – not complete sets, but enough to protect them. Dhara too, had worn, rather hastily, a set of armor. Galene herself had her pendant. But Caelus…

Take care, thought Galene, cutting down another opponent.

Then looked at her target. "Cardea!" she yelled, furious. "Come and face me, you coward!"

"Why should I do that, young Helianov?" she questioned, her clear voice carrying over sounds of blood and carnage. "I am clearly winning!"

Galene snorted. "Think again, lady – you're going down."

Cardea laughed. "Correct your count, Helianov," she said, spitting the title like it was an insult. Raising one of her twin hunting knives, which she had been holding down lazily, she cut down at one of the Phoenixes that flew around the room at a new opponent. The Yttra fell down, shattering on impact as though he had become ice. "That would be thirteen. The odds are stacked against you. Surrender, and you will suffer less."

Galene glared. "I already have, traitor!" she yelled, sending a stream of Blackfire at her enemies, clearing a path for her to Cardea. "You murdered my grandfather!"

Cardea waved a hand as though it was nothing. "He was asking for it."

"Argh!" Galene threw a ball of Darkfire at Cardea. She batted it aside with her blade, charring it. "§*Soulfire*§!" Galene commanded. The Pyrós glowed brightly, shooting out a stream of dark flames. All around them, the sounds of battle ceased, and all the creatures, both Cardea's and the Heleanovan, retreated.

"Darkfire?" murmured Aura, tilting her head.

Another flame shot out from the still glowing blade – Heartfire – and intertwined itself with the first, both covering Cardea in it's fiery embrace. Then came Shadowfire, ready to fulfill her promise.

And now came a green flame – Stormfire. Fire and Water – and the two spun around in a deadly dance. The fire joined the cage around Cardea, now hidden by the raging inferno.

Here came the next flame – Blackfire, of her anger. It entered the cage, ready for vengeance.

But it wasn't so.

With a wild scream, Cardea threw open her arms and, with a blast of energy, destroyed the cage. As the energy rolled over her, Galene fell to her knees. *That…what is that?* She thought, feeling nausea rolling off her.

The answer came to her in a second.

"Chaos," whispered Galene, horrified. Barely glancing at the others, she whispered a quick prayer to Pyra for protection, and pulled her pendant.

From the insignia, the lone flame spread to cover her entire body, forming an armor to rival the works of the Ancient Smiths[1].

1 After they created the People, the Elements gathered a group of the most skilled blacksmiths, and got from them five sets of armor. This they gave to each of the Heleanova. The armor was light and smooth, rumored to never rust, never fade – simply exist for all Heleanova to use.

The Pyrós appeared in its sheath at her waist, and in her hands appeared two double-bladed swords – the Ignis and the Glac. Gifts from Pyra and Hedro.

Rising, she spun the blades in her hands as she approached Cardea. "You are truly Gvan," she whispered, horrified by her acts. "You have become-"

"Chaotic?" asked Cardea, laughing. "It was the small price he asked in exchange for his help."

"Help?" demanded Galene, incredulous. "What're you trying to do, destroy the worlds?"

Cardea raised an eyebrow. "What has the world done for me?" She questioned.

"The worlds, Cardea," snapped Galene. "They're the reason you exist. They are the source of all non-chaotic magic – the source of the Elements. Unless…" She tapered off, horrified by the possibility. "That's what you're after. The destruction of the Elements."

"Exactly," said Cardea. "They have created the People, yes, but what else? They have not helped us progress-"

"Because of the Laws-" Interrupted Galene.

"That they wrote!" snapped Cardea, waving an arm. "They decided against helping-"

"Against interfering!" Galene yelled, frustrated. "If the Elements interfered, Chaos would have won!"

"And would that be so terrible?" She asked.

"Yes!" said Galene. "The Elements are the reason we still exist. Without them, we would be chaos – no individuals. No I, not even an us – just Chaos."

"You are being close minded, as you were taught. No matter – you will soon realize the truth."

"This is the truth!" Galene shouted, spinning the Glac. "Chaos leads to nothing but murder and death."

Cardea looked at her pitying. "Andres Alwood was a great man. It was a necessary sacrifice."

"It wasn't necessary, and it wasn't a sacrifice. It was murder, pure and simple."

Cardea shook her head. "It was necessary, Galene. He was powerful, but misguided. He would have stopped me, I am not ashamed to admit it."

Galene straightened her shoulders, narrowing her eyes. Vesta flashed onto her shoulder in a jet of fire, and the other Heleanova stood by her with their Arra. "Then you should have killed us as well."

And with that, the battle resumed.

Galene attacked Cardea, slashing with the two swords.

Cardea parried every strike with her hunting knives, rarely going on the offensive. Galene didn't give her much chance of that. Here a slash with one blade of the Ignis, and there a stab with the Glac, followed by a sweep of both, at different places, all aiming to wound, if not worse.

But Cardea's twin blades, flashing with Chaotic magic – a meld of warring Elements – intercepted each cut.

Warring Elements…

With a feral grin, she threw at Cardea a ball of Fire and Water, coexisting and fighting together, rather than against each other. *Perhaps that is the key?* Thought Galene, spinning the Glac to send a gale of icy water at Cardea.

Galene shook her head. *No,* she thought. She remembered a small story she had read in "The True Fire" – a legend that had gotten distorted with time. They say that Chaos was tired of fighting for so long, and he surrendered – but could a being that has no concept of time get tired of a long war? No, it seemed unlikely. Chaos was the creator, and that he would be tired due to some strands of temporary conscience – it seemed inconceivable.

What really happened was Fire's Fury. She was always short tempered and impatient. In a fit of anger, she attacked Chaos head on. She did not succeed, but in the attempt, Water had been wounded. Intent on revenge, she attacked once more. But this time, she was careful. Instead of letting her anger take over her senses, she used it to fuel her powers. And with this new strength, with Fire's Fury, she struck a blow that freed the Riella from Chaos, though they did not realize it.

But Chaos did, and he 'conceded', waiting for the right moment to strike. He did so during The Elemental War, before the People were created. The world began to dissolve into chaos, because he willed it. He used the part of him that had been in the five Riella, and slowly pulled the world apart. When Ether intervened, Fire realized her sickness, and, overwhelmed with guilt and shame, fled afar. It was only several years later that she returned and helped create the People. She cleansed herself of the Chaos that was in her, and never spoke of it again. Until one of her Heleanova asked the question – how?

This is why Fire is considered the Purest Element – yes, rash, and harsh, but pure. Because she is the only one who realized, and the only one who removed the Chaos.

And this means, thought Galene gleefully, *he can't control me. And so she can't either.*

And when Cardea broke out of her cage, she was prepared.

She didn't fight with Fire and Water, but with Pure Fire. Unchaotic.

"You think that will help you, Helianov?" demanded Cardea, glaring. "It will not help." Her eyes were no longer the pale blue of the Vrar Heleanova. They were pure black, darker than the darkest shadow, darker than the deepest night –

so dark that it seemed that no flame could dispel it. Her powers over the other Elements became this dark ire, seeming to destroy any hope all around the world.

It reached Caelus first, and, despite his fire, he couldn't hold on. It brought him to his knees, slowly dragging her fellow Heleanova down, hopeless with despair.

Burn with my fire, my Helianov, said a voice in her head. Pyra.

Galene recalled the insignia – the fire of Pyra, the lone flame that burns brightest when it seems all hope has been lost.

"It will help," she whispered softly. "It will, because I am ve fa Pyra. The Pure." With that, she raised her swords, and ordered, "§*Soulfire*§!" This time, the flames enveloped her blades, her armor – everything burned bright, dispelling the dark despair around them.

Her six flames – Darkfire, Blackfire, Shadowfire, Heartfire, Stormfire and Pyra's fire – her Soulfire. They burned brightly, and slowly, but surely, Chaos retreated.

"Leave, Chaos!" yelled Galene, her voice carrying over the crackling of her Fire. "You have no business here, and no chance against Fire's Fury!"

Cardea took one look at Galene's eyes, and fled. Chaos had lost.

And with that knowledge, Galene lost conscience.

CHAPTER 27

The first thing that she heard was arguing voices.

"-She is sleeping!"

"She owes us-"

"Nothing!" snapped the first voice.

"She should-"

"Sleep!"

Galene groaned. "A little late for that, isn't it?" she questioned.

"Galene!" cried the first voice.

"Miss Alwood!" came the second.

"Stop shouting," snapped Galene.

Aura came into her vision. "Well, Galene, you should have thought of that before you decided to burn the city down."

Galene's eyes widened. "Burn the city down?"

"Not really, just the street." Caelus entered the room, sidestepping someone vaguely familiar. "You lost control when you became unconscious."

Galene stared at the third person. "Elethia?" questioned Galene, incredulous. "What are you doing here?"

She held her nose high. "Waiting for an explanation."

Galene shook her head. "I'm a bit tired. Dhara," she called, looking at him as he entered. "I recall explaining something to you after we collected the Kÿma. Would you be so kind as to explain that to Elethia?"

Dhara grinned. "Of course," he said. "With pleasure." He turned to Elethia. "Let's get something straight, officer Elethia. We don't owe you anything, explanation or otherwise. If you're curious, then *ask*. Don't *demand*. Knowing is not your right, and you certainly can't demand it. If we want to, or feel the need to answer your questions, then you'll get your answer. Otherwise, you might just find yourself on the wrong side of something powerful, and you'll regret it."

Elethia's eyes narrowed. "Is that a threat?"

"No," began Dhara.

"It's a certainty." The Heleanova finished in unison.

Elethia's eyes widened, and she backed out of the room quickly, nearly tripping over her boots as she left.

In three seconds, the five teens began laughing. "Word-for-word!" gasped Galene between laughs. "How did you remember?"

Dhara straightened. "It was rather difficult to forget."

"So, what happened?"

"You destroyed most of the creatures there. I think your Nerra is your heart."

"Vesta?" she asked, fearfully.

I am a being of fire, Galene, Vesta informed her. *It would take more than fire to destroy me. Or perhaps less.*

Galene laughed. "Get here, little bird." Vesta trilled in anger, and swooped over the bed swiftly. Galene shook her head. "Ok, Vesta. Not a little bird."

She trilled in satisfaction, and settled near her bed.

"Where am I?" Asked Galene, after petting Vesta for a bit.

"In officer Draven's place."

"What!"

Caelus rolled his eyes. "He offered. He lives ten streets from there. It was virtually untouched by the fire."

"And the people who lived nearby?"

"Everybody survived."

"What's the worst injury?"

"A second degree burn on the arm. To Elethia."

"And she fusses so," said Aura. "It saved her life – she'd been infected by Chaos. A few burns set that right, but does she care? Nope."

"How long was I out?" interjected Galene, cutting off Aura's rant.

"Two days."

Galene winced. Two days? A lot could happen.

"But, no harm done. Now you tell us. What happened?"

Galene smiled at Caelus. "Chaos got burned. Literally."

Caelus rolled his eyes. "Somehow, we got that part, but how?"

Galene sighed, and began her explanation. At the end of it, Despione raised an eyebrow. "How do we get pure?"

Galene shrugged. "Fire's power resides in her Fury. You need to find yours."

And find them they will.

THE END